Dear Mr. Albert, ...*It's Me, Prince!*

Narrated by Prince

(Written with a little help from sisters
**Sabrina "Sage" Ginsburg,
Sophie "Paris" Ginsburg,**
and family)

Illustrator: Elena Jacobson

Series: DEAR MR. ALBERT, Book 1
Print and Illustrations © 2018 Keshare Inc.
All rights reserved.
ISBN-13: 9780999740309
ISBN-10: 099974030X
Library of Congress Control Number: 2017919717
Keshare Inc., Lake Worth

This book is dedicated to
The Martin County Correctional Institute
B.A.R.K. Program

Dogs 4 Disabled Veterans (D4DV) is a nonprofit organization that is committed to the rehabilitation of rescue dogs and to giving them a purpose as service dogs or emotional support dogs for disabled veterans. They are located in South Florida and proudly serve veterans throughout the state.

D4DV works in partnership with the Martin Correctional Institute through a Train-the-Trainer program called B.A.R.K. (Beacon Among Rescued K9s).

www.dogs4disabledveterans.org

A portion of the *Dear Mr. Albert, ...It's Me, Prince!* book proceeds will be donated to the Train-the-Trainer program, B.A.R.K.

Much gratitude to Marilyn Rudne and Susan Gurspan for their guidance in editing this book and to the students and teaching professionals that participated in our focus groups. All of your contributions have been priceless.

From the Voice of Prince

Dear Mr. Albert, ...It's Me, Prince! is designed for classroom study. Students will be exposed to what it's like for an animal or person to have a disability while increasing their vocabulary and learning overall life lessons through Prince's adventures.

This story is based on real-life characters.

TABLE OF CONTENTS

This book belongs to: _____

Other people who have read my book:

_____

_____

_____

_____

_____

_____

Prince is very excited for you to read his story!

DOGS 4 DISABLED VETERANS PROGRAM

Prince graduated at the top of his class when training for the Dogs 4 Disabled Veterans (D4DV) program. He worked in partnership with the Florida Department of Corrections at the Martin Correctional Work Camp and was enrolled in the Train-the-Trainer program, called B.A.R.K. Prince was trained by an inmate. Service dogs like Prince are in training anywhere from two to three years, depending on which behaviors need to be worked on. This is a win-win-win program. It's a win for the dog that's being rescued and given a second chance at a good life. It's a win for the inmate who learns a trade that will help keep him out of the prison system. It's also a win for our disabled veterans who bravely gave of themselves in service to our country.

Most of Prince's friends in the program became official service dogs who help disabled veterans with their daily lives. They assist with everyday tasks, such as opening and closing doors, helping get someone dressed, and much, much more. Below are just some of the special types of incredible service dogs:

- *Hearing dogs* assist hearing-impaired or deaf people.
- *Visual dogs* help visually impaired or blind people.
- *Mobility assistance dogs* assist people in wheel-chairs and more.
- *Seizure response dogs* aid people with seizures.
- *Mental health service dogs* assist people with post-traumatic stress disorder, panic disorders, anxiety disorders, major depression, autism spectrum disorders, and much more.

LETTER ONE

Dear Mr. Albert,

It's me, Prince! I'm really sorry I haven't written to you sooner, but I wanted to wait until I really knew what it was like to live at my new house with the family who adopted me.

I've been here about two months, and I can officially say I feel like I'm home. I'm learning a lot... *like how to use big words*, which you will see when I write to you. I miss the prison* where you and I spent time together in the program that taught dogs like me to help disabled* veterans.* Given everything that I learned, I still can't believe I won't be placed in a home to help a person who needs a wheelchair or someone who has trouble hearing. But I won't forget

* **Prison** is a place where people who have broken the law must live to make up for the bad thing(s) they have done. People who go to prison may have to stay for months, years, or even a lifetime. Prison is also called a jail or a correctional facility.

* **Disabled** is when someone is affected by an illness or injury. Some disabilities can be easy to see, such as when someone must use a wheelchair. But disabilities in people or animals may not always be visible.

* A **veteran** is a person who served as a member of the armed forces and is now retired. Veterans protected our country and are highly respected for their service.

anything you taught me. I'm so happy to be out of the hospital. As you know, I was there three months before they figured out what was wrong with me. BTW (by the way), *my disability is called Addison's disease.*

Okay—so after the hospital, I was in a couple of different foster homes*, which were really nice, but none ever quite felt like this place. I can't wait to tell you all about it. Ms. Becky, who helped teach our training program, came to check on me

* Foster home is a temporary place for animals or children to live while being cared for by people or a family who have volunteered to take care of them.

3

the first day I was here. I was super happy to see her. She went over all of my special needs with my new family and hung out with us for a while. She was very complimentary* about all that you taught me and how well you cared for me. I haven't forgotten everything, but with my condition, I'm not really being asked to use all of my commands—just a few to keep good communication between me and my new folks.

So where do I begin? Ah, yes, at my new home, I have a puppy brother whose

* Complimentary is an expression used when explaining you liked what someone did.

name is Bailey, and he's a mix of Maltese and Poodle. He's four years old. We can get a little crazy together with all of our toys, and he doesn't seem to mind sharing. Oh, and my new family bought me all kinds of fun toys of my own! We play tug-of-war with our rope toy, and we fetch a

ball together with our family in the back-yard. So fun!

Mr. Albert, I must say my mom and dad are always making sure I feel good and have everything I need. Oh, Mom and Dad said they're going to try to get a fence so Bailey and I can run around like crazy every day. OMG (oh my goodness), I can't wait! Bailey is the best older brother ever! Even though I'm taller than he is, I still look up to him. After all, he's almost three years older than I am. He has a lot more doggy wisdom* than I do. Oh, the pool at my new house is very different from the pool at the prison you and I lived at,

* **Wisdom** is knowledge gained from life experiences and learning from them.

Mr. Albert. My new pool is in the ground and soooo... big compared to the plastic baby pool I used to play in.

Mr. Albert, I'm just realizing how much I didn't see of the outside world when I lived with you in the prison. What I do know is that you cared so much about me and taught me so much when I was there. The program I was in, which used inmates,* like you, to train service dogs for dis-abled veterans, was very special. Y'know, I think it taught us both good behavior,

* **Inmates** are people who live in jail or a correctional facility because they broke the law. They are separated from family and friends.

7

right? One thing I noticed was that some of my other dog friends at the prison were able to spend their weekends at nearby private homes to experience what life was like on the outside. As you know, I never was able to do that because I got so sick.

I hope you're still working with dogs. The humans, like Ms. Becky, who put this program together did such a *GREAT* job. They made sure that the trainers, like you, were kind, had good behavior, and had *no* record of cruelty* to animals.

* Cruelty is when an animal or person is treated very badly.

TBH (to be honest), I can't imagine there being any better program than the Dogs 4 Disabled Veterans B.A.R.K. program that I graduated from. I still remember how to open doors and drawers as well as many of my commands, like "back up." I still like fetching things for people. I heard Ms. Becky made some cool videos of me and some other dogs training! Maybe we'll become famous someday. Woo-hoo bark, bark!

Oh, did I mention that since I came to live in the real world, I have been told my bark is very annoying, when I get excited?

LOL (laughing out loud). My bark is very high pitched for a medium-sized dog of twenty pounds. My little squirrel girlfriend loves♥ it, though. She, too, makes a cute noise when she's eating. It's hard for me to explain, but I love♥ to sit upright and listen to her munch on her acorns.

I also have two human sisters who are twelve and fourteen years old. I can tell they're crazy about *me*. BTW, they both love❤ when I hang out with them.

My mom also has a medical condition and has to give herself a shot from time to time. My dad is a pharmacist, so between the two of them, they don't mind giving me my shot every month and my pill every other day.

I still can't believe I have Addison's disease, but I'm really living life pretty well, considering I have to be careful about being in the heat and other things. Do you know what Addison's disease is, Mr. Albert? It has to do with something called hormones* in your body and your adrenal glands.* Humans can have this condition, too. My medicine makes me drink a lot of water, and my mom and dad bought me this great water fountain to drink from. It has a filter, so the water always tastes really good, and my mom knows how much I love♥ ice cubes!

Guess what else my mom and dad give me and Bailey? Ice cubes made from

* Hormones are chemicals in animal and human blood that control certain cell and organ functions.
* Adrenal glands are located on top of each kidney in both animals and humans. If glands in our bodies are working properly, they help keep us healthy.

chicken soup! Yup, *real soup,* which is even sometimes homemade! It's yummy! They feed me really well; they buy me grain-free food. Sometimes I eat wet food, but other times they give me dry food with water and heat it up a little in the micro-wave. I love❤ the smell of it when it gets heated up. *Delish!* They also buy me grain-free doggy treats and always have plenty of fresh carrots and apples on hand for me to snack on.

Mom can't eat grains either; she calls it eating "gluten-free."* It's a special diet.

---

* Gluten-free is a special diet in which wheat and grains, including barley, rye, oat, and more, are not eaten.

I think I get a little pesty when I see her eating sometimes. I just can't help myself because her food looks so good, and I know I can eat it safely without getting a tummy ache. *You know me*—if I eat something that doesn't agree with me, I end up eating grass, and the grass makes me throw up. Oh, but then I end up eating my throw up, so it's all good! LOL. My sisters think it's totally yucky when I do this. Ha-ha.

Ta-ta for now. Lick (kiss), lick (kiss), woof, wooof.

LETTER TWO

Dear Mr. Albert,

My dad works from our house many days on his computer, and my fave (favorite) thing to do while he's working is to lie in my bed and hang out next to him. He uses a room in our house for his office. Bailey also has a bed in the office, and we often have a staring contest before we nap in the afternoon.

Usually, Dad gives us each a bone to chew on after we nap in the afternoon, and I've been surprisingly good about leaving Bailey's alone and just gnawing on my own. Still, sometimes I just can't help myself. Normally, I finish my bone in about three seconds. Since I'm almost always hungry for something to eat, the next best thing is to eat Bailey's bone. I just have to be patient enough to wait for him to look the other way, and then I sneak in and *grab it*! But sometimes, I'm lucky. He just walks away, and I can get it easily.

Really, though, my fave treat is an authentic* deer antler. Not to worry— they're naturally shed from deer, and once they're picked up from the ground, they're cleaned really well. My new doc- tor told us about them. As you know, I love❤ to chew on bones, but this antler

* Authentic is something that's real; it's not fake or pretend.

dog treat is better than a bone! It lasts me a couple of months or more. Bailey has one, too.

Mr. Albert, I must tell you about the new veterinarian* place where I go. It has an outside water park for dogs my size and smaller, and it also has a doggy hotel, so I can go on vacation just like my parents do. The workers there take really good care of the dogs. I love❤ the spa there, where I get a relaxing massage and bath at the same time, and the oatmeal shampoo they use smells so good. I still get

* A **veterinarian** is a doctor who takes care of animals.

my teeth brushed, just not every day like you used to do, but I don't really care. Ah, it's getting late. Good night. I'll write you again soon.

Ta-ta for now. Lick, lick, woof, wooof.

LETTER THREE

Dear Mr. Albert,

I usually walk around my neighborhood at least twice a day with Bailey and either Mom and Dad or my sisters. We walk in the early morning and then again when the sun goes down at night, so I don't get overheated. There is a sidewalk in my neighborhood. I'm pretty good about staying on it, but I can get a little distracted when I see all the kids in the neighborhood on their bikes and skateboards. I'm always on my leash, so even if I'm tempted to get myself into trouble, I stay well mannered.

There are lots of other dogs in our neighborhood, and they're all very friendly. I felt really bad after meeting one of them for the first time. Her name is Scoop. I was a little nervous to be around her 'cause she's really friendly and very pretty, and I accidentally went pee on her. Yikes! Everyone just laughed it off, but I was a little embarrassed. Whoopsie! But I just kept thinking to myself, *La-di-dah,* la-di-dah, I can stay nonchalant* about this and not skip a beat. Just keep walking. And that's exactly what I did!

If you want me to (and I'm sure·you do), I'll continue to write you and let you know how things are going. I hope you're doing okay. I heard you're training a new puppy named Rusty and that you may get to go home soon. I think of you often. Pleeeeeeeeze... know I'm in a really great place and that I'll always be grateful* to you for everything you did for me. I

---

* **Nonchalant** is relaxed or calm in a way that shows you're not worried about anything.

* **Grateful** is a feeling of being thankful.

know it was really hard when I got sick and they had to rush me away to the hospital. The good news is that I'm doing well, and I'm so, so happy and feel so loved❤ where I'm living. I'll write and tell you more real soon.

Ta-ta for now. Lick, lick, woof, wooof.

LETTER FOUR

Dear Mr. Albert,

Well, as promised, I'm writing you again.
I have so, so much to share. Let me back
up a little and tell you all the details of how
I arrived at my "forever home." Forgive
me if I get distracted from time to time.
Sometimes I can't concentrate for very
long, as I'm pretty hyper. My mind just
jumps around a lot, which you probably

remember about me. What can I say? I was born this way! I like to daydream a lot, and it's fun.

I'll tell you everything, but it just may be a little discombobulated.* I just love♥ the word "dis...com...bob...u...la...ted." You should try saying it out loud. I'm also trying to learn what bigger words mean and actually use them. If you don't understand something I write, just look at the bottom of the letter for help in understanding the definitions of my big words.

* Discombobulated is when things are mixed up, not in order, confusing.

"Discombobulate" is Prince's fave word!

Oh, and I want to tell you that I didn't come straight home to the house I'm living in. After leaving the animal hospital, I first went to a foster home. They were really nice people, but they had a very fancy home, and I could tell they didn't want me to go into certain rooms.

The name of the lady of the home was Mrs. Piper, and she worked at an office where she took me every day. At the office, I met this amazing lady named Ms. Judi. She and so many other ladies loved♥ to hang out with me, but there was something special about Ms. Judi. She kept talking to someone on the phone about me and telling them how cute and sweet I was. Ms. Judi was a funny lady; she would talk to me nonstop and say things like, "Hello, Prince; you're such a cutie patootie...oh, how my Bailey would like to be friends with you." I wondered who Bailey was and if I would really like him.

I was sort of like a celebrity* at the office, and they asked me to be in a commercial; that was so much fun. I think

* A celebrity is an animal or person who is famous or very well known.

the commercial ended up being on TV. I

held a phone in my mouth at the end of

the commercial, and people were told

to call a certain number if they needed

help. It was a number to call for help

for senior citizens, homeless* people, and

* **Homeless** is when an animal or person has no place to live and therefore often ends up living on the streets.

anyone who might be having a crisis.* It was a free phone call for any human, and I can tell you they really do help people all day and night. I sat next to some of the ladies that answered the phones.

One lady answered the phone for someone who was homeless and needed to find a place to eat. They found her a soup kitchen* right away. This made me so happy, but I was also sad when I thought about the many dogs and even cats out on the streets that could use this type of help. Maybe

* A **crisis** is a difficult or dangerous situation that needs serious attention.
* A **soup kitchen** is a place where food (such as soup and bread) is given to poor people.

homeless animals needed a soup kitchen. Um... I wonder if there is such a thing for animals that don't have families and live on the streets. Come to think of it, I think one of the other dogs that I trained with came from an animal shelter. Maybe that was a place that helped dogs in crisis.

One day, at the office, I heard Mrs. Piper and Ms. Judi talking about a place I might like to live. I was scared because that's the place where Bailey lived. I was worried that if that family already had a dog, they wouldn't love❤ me as much.

I wanted to end up in a home where I would be loved♥ unconditionally.* Y'know Mr. Albert, I loved♥ you unconditionally. I know you were put in prison because you got into trouble with the law, but I'm certain that when you get out and have a second chance at life, you will be a good citizen.* Maybe you can write me back and let me know what you end up doing when you leave the prison.

I'll check the mailbox every day, just in case you write me. You can count on me to write you again real soon.

Ta-ta for now. Lick, lick, woof, wooof.

* Unconditionally is when you love♥ someone or something no matter what.
* A citizen is a person who lives in a particular place or country.

LETTER FIVE

Dear Mr. Albert,

A few days have passed since I've written. I totally forgot to tell you so much before. No worries. I won't leave any details out. Okeydokey, this story makes me smile so *big.* It happened before I knew for sure that I had found my forever family.

Okay, so I remember walking down the street in my foster family's pish-posh neighborhood, and along came a smiley lady with a big nose; a tall, broad-shouldered man; and a fluffy little white dog. The dog was wagging his tail very fast, and I was hoping we could stop and meet them all. Sure enough, Mrs. Piper and her husband walked me straight toward them. We all stopped, and I started sniffing this cute fluffy little white dog. After a few sniffs, we started playing around, and then we all started walking together down this beautiful street. The street had tall palm trees, and I could see the ocean water in the distance. It was a very sunny day, and there was a slight breeze in the air. I had my head up high, so I could feel the wind in my nose. I was so happy! I was just thinking to myself, *this is such a great day. Shucks!* And that day I thought, *if only I could find a family that would take me for walks like this all the time.*

Well, sure enough, the fluffy white dog and I started skipping alongside one another, and the four adults were walking and talking. Before I knew it, our leashes were tangled up, because we were having so much fun together. I heard the smiley lady say, "Bailey, sit." I could not believe it! I thought to myself, could this be the Bailey that Ms. Judi talked about in the office? Could it be? Could it really be? Did she really make this happen? Clearly, Mr. Albert, you know what happened, but let me finish the story anyway. As we walked closer to the water where there was a little park, the four adults stopped to let us play. It was amazing to have met Bailey, and all I could think about was that maybe this could be my new family!

After about an hour, we all walked back toward the house I was staying in, and Mrs. Piper invited us in to visit. We all went inside, and Bailey started sniffing around the house. I was searching for my tennis ball when I looked over and saw that Bailey was going pee... on the leg

of Mrs. Piper's good chair. Oops! Mrs.

Piper was very nice about it. Personally,

I thought it was pretty funny because

Mrs. Piper was a little uptight about

keeping her home so perfect. I heard

Mrs. Piper tell her husband that when

I left, another dog would come to stay

with them. I think it was her son's dog. I sure hoped that dog was ready to live in a house that looked like it should be in a magazine every day.

It was like what I imagined a palace to look like. Well...a small palace. *Don't get me wrong*—the house was beautiful but just not comfy for me. After all, I'm a jock, a sporty type of dog. I like to get a little wild and crazy, as you know, Mr. Albert. Even though I don't shed, I may bring in some dirt or a lizard from sniffing around outside. That's just my thing. Gotta love❤ those Florida lizards. I think they may be called geckos. They do make for a good snack from time to time. I'm just licking my lips thinking about it. YumMMMmmmMMMM. Ha-ha, I just actually caught myself drooling a little. Okay, time for my afternoon nap. I remember dreaming about what my new family might be like. As always, I'll write you again.

Ta-ta for now. Lick, lick, woof, wooof.

LETTER SIX

Dear Mr. Albert,

Okay, so when I woke up from my nap, I could see that my dog crate, canned foods, toys, and even my medications were being gathered up and put by Mrs. Piper's front door. My heart was pounding, and I started B-A-R-K-I-N-G a little out of excitement. I just needed to know I was not dreaming and that I was actually awake. I remember asking myself if

Mr. Ken, Mrs. Melanie, and Bailey would be taking me home to live with them. I wondered if their house would be fancy like this one. All the carpets in Mrs. Piper's house were white, and there was lots of furniture that I could not sit on. I had also wondered if Mrs. Piper and her husband even knew that I didn't shed or drool much and that I knew better than to chew on anything in the house. After all, Mr. Albert, you taught me well. Phew-wee.

Okay, let me get back on track. I went over and put my front paws on the windowsill so I could see out the window, and I

saw a nice white car pull up to the house.
Bingo! Mr. Ken was putting my stuff
into the car. OMG, I thought to myself.
Could it be? Could this be happening? Was
I officially being adopted? Or would it
be another foster home? Mr. Ken then
came into the house and put my leash
on. He was a large-built man, and when I
looked at him, he was a little intimidating*
in his dark sunglasses. But I could tell that
he was just a big teddy bear on the inside.
Mr. Ken, whom I hoped I would soon call

* Intimidating is something that makes you frightened or scared.

my dad, walked me to the car and asked me to sit in the back with all of my stuff. I was a little nervous getting into this car. Yet the people I was pretty sure I would call my new forever parents were very affectionate.* Mrs. Melanie looked back at me and said, "Prince you're going to be the happiest dog ever!" She told me not to be nervous and held my paw for the entire ride in the car.

After a short car ride, I heard Mr. Ken say, "Let's take Prince for a walk

* **Affectionate** is showing warmth and kindness to someone or something that you really like or love❤. Affection is communicated by words, gestures, or touches.

around his new neighborhood so he can check it out. Then we'll take him to the house, his new home." At that point, I knew I was going to soon see my new house! We parked in front of a beautiful lake and took a walk around it. They let me sniff whatever I wanted. Everyone I saw in the neighborhood was looking at me, and they smiled and asked who I was.

I tried to walk with confidence,* although I was very eager to see where

---

* **Confidence** is a feeling of pride and of being certain of yourself or your actions.

we were going. Eventually, we walked up to a two-story house with a black garage door. They opened the garage door, and on one side of the garage was an orange Jeep, which didn't have a top on it. It was a convertible. I had seen many of these cars, since we live in Florida, but I had never ridden in one. I was hoping that I would get to ride in that car real soon! Then the door to the house opened, and I started B-A-R-K-I-N-G like crazy, so Mr. Ken leaned down, took my leash off, and let me go. I couldn't hold back my excitement!

I didn't know what to look at first. This house was much different from Mrs. Piper's. This house had lots of colors on the walls, and the sofa was dark brown. It was so warm and cheerful. Then I could see two girls heading in from out back. They opened the sliding glass door, and the smaller one came running over to me and hugged me. She said, "Who is this?" The taller girl looked at me and almost started crying and seemed confused about me being there. Uh-oh. Mr. Ken and

Mrs. Melanie then explained to them who I was and said that I was an early holiday present.

Paris, the younger of the two sisters, was overwhelmed* with happiness; I could really tell she was happy because one thing you taught me, Mr. Albert, was how important people's facial expressions are. Sage, the older of the two sisters was not as happy with me being there, at first; she was apprehensive.* After a few minutes, I went up to Sage and licked her face all over and smiled at her. She had medium-brown long hair, and her face

* Overwhelmed is when an animal or person has too many emotions; it can be a positive or negative feeling.
* Apprehensive is when you feel uneasy or scared causing nervousness.

had lots of freckles. I just wanted to lick every one of them. I think she could tell how much I liked her, and before long, she started stroking my back and saying hello. Her voice crackled a little bit as she petted me. Paris, on the other hand, was very enthusiastic* and had already figured out I liked fetching a tennis ball, so we immediately started playing together. Paris was sweet and friendly with long, thick curly brown hair and hazel-greenish eyes.

As Mr. Ken was bringing all my stuff into the house from the car, I heard him

* Enthusiastic is when you feel excited and very interested in something.

say that Ms. Becky, our trainer from the prison, would be coming over the next day.

Mr. Ken also said that Ms. Becky needed to see the house I was staying in. Here I was all excited about the possibility of being in my new home, and Ms. Becky could decide to take that away from me. Yet I knew her so well, right, Mr. Albert? So, I took a deep breath; held my tongue out, with my mouth open wide; and told myself that it would be okay. I knew Ms. Becky would only want the best for me. She was the nicest, most patient lady I had ever met in my life. She loved♥ dogs more than humans, I think. That night, I had a hard time sleeping.

The very next day, Ms. Becky rang the doorbell. When I greeted her, she got down on one knee and kissed me. I jumped up on her, put my two front paws on her shoulders and hugged her. It was so good to see her, but when I saw her, it really made me miss you, and I was a little sad that day. Ms. Becky immediately started using some of my commands. It felt like old times. It was so nice hanging out with Ms. Becky. Mr. Albert, I hope you like all my stories of how I found my forever family. I'm so happy that Mrs. Melanie and Mr. Ken turned out to be my parents and that they were able to meet Ms. Becky. Maybe they'll meet you someday, too.

Ta-ta for now. Lick, lick, woof, wooof.

LETTER SEVEN

Dear Mr. Albert,

A few days later, I kept hearing my mom say that my name should be Bailey, and my brother Bailey's name should be Prince. Why? Well, my brother Bailey always seems to be acting like a prince. He doesn't like to get dirty; when we go on family walks, he has to step around the puddles or any dirt on the sidewalk. I, on the other hand, *love*❤ to sniff around for things that may have died in the grass and to roll around in those spots. Since I still live in Florida, there are many lizards and worms in the grass that I like to look for. I love❤ to chase lizards around, and if I catch them, I like to eat them or at least part of them.

Bailey didn't think that was a good idea when he saw me do this at first, but then after a while, he started doing it too. I think it's terrific that he's starting to do things like me. He was always such a Goody-Two-Shoes. Don't get me wrong, Mr. Albert; I'm still really well behaved, I think. It's just that since I left the hospital and found my new home, I haven't been using my commands as much. I think it's because of my Addison's disease. I guess everything happens for a reason though. If I didn't have this disease, I would have never met my forever family. Not that I want to be sick, but I seriously feel like this is the house I'm meant to be living in.

I also have two sets of grandparents who live close by. Lou Lou and Poppy are my mom's parents, and Dee Dee and Pops are my dad's parents. Dee Dee and Pops have a dog named Teddy, and he's Bailey's real brother. So cool. I just found out he will be visiting us for three weeks. I'm excited because Teddy actually plays with me more than Bailey does.

I've heard the story about when Mom and Dad adopted Bailey. They took Dee Dee and Pops with them, and Dee Dee fell in love❤ with Teddy and begged Pops for a puppy. Their dog had passed away a few months earlier, and Dee Dee really missed having a dog in the house. Pops really didn't want another dog, but he gave in. Now he's so crazy in love❤ with Teddy, and I can see why.

Mom and Dad agreed when they adopted Bailey that when Dee Dee and Pops traveled, Teddy would stay at our house. Boy, do Dee Dee and Pops travel a lot, but it's fine by me! Now sometimes Bailey gets a little jealous of my relation-ship with Teddy and growls at me for no reason when Teddy is visiting. TBH, I think it's pretty hilarious, and I just ignore him. Sometimes Teddy takes up for himself and starts growling back at Bailey, and they growl so loudly and hard that their teeth show.

Geez, I really need to go potty. Gotta run. Thank goodness my doggy door is open. Out I go!

Ta-ta for now. Lick, lick, woof, wooof.

LETTER EIGHT

Dear Mr. Albert,

You may be wondering if I've been going to the doctor. I want you to know that Mom and Dad started giving me my shots instead of taking me to the doctor every three weeks. Mom is really good at it. The nurse at the vet's office taught her how to do it. Mom is very gentle and always talks to me to tell me she's almost finished.

Dad holds me tight, while Mom gives me my shot. I think I drive them crazy the day I'm due for my shot because I start to get into things. I crave paper, so I go from one garbage can to another looking for paper and anything else I can possibly eat and tear apart. I must admit, I can make a really *big* mess if they don't catch me in time.

I have to fast-forward a few months. Mom has really not been feeling well and could not help me journal as much to you, Mr. Albert. So I decided to start keeping track of things that have happened by myself, although I have a very *big* imagination. I'll leave it up to you, Mr. Albert, to decide if what I'm writing is really happening or if my imagination is running wild. Bark, bark...oh, and I just had a little gas. Oh no! Now it stinks in here. I sometimes chase my tail trying to smell my own farts. Yeah, yeah, I know that's gross, but seriously, I can be grosser. My name really should be changed- hey, maybe I should change it to Pew....—wee. But no, I like being called Prince; it makes me feel important. Time to go on my walk and strut my stuff around the neighborhood. Write you again soon.

Ta-ta for now. Lick, lick, woof, wooof.

LETTER NINE

Dear Mr. Albert,

When I woke up today, it was pour-ing rain and thundering really loud. It made me think about Teddy because he really doesn't like thunder. You know one thing you taught me, Mr. Albert, was how to pick up a phone, and I've since learned how to dial phone numbers. I called Dee Dee and Pops to check on Teddy. I was hoping Teddy would answer the phone, but Dee

Dee did. Dee Dee is always so surprised to hear me on the other end of the phone when I call. (You'd think she would be used to it by now.) I heard Teddy barking in the background to speak with me. When he finally got on the phone, he told me he was a nervous wreck about the thunderstorm and hoped it would pass soon. I reminded him to put on his special thunder shirt because it helps calm him down.

Later on that day, the rain had stopped, and the sun came out really bright. I had just come back into the house through my doggy door when in walked the biggest surprise ever- my cousins from Louisville, Kentucky! My cousin Armand came running through the door yelling, "Prince, Prince—wuzzup?" My cousins were so funny and spoke with real southern accents. So when he said "wuzzup," it was really like "wu...zz... UP...!"

I barked back at him, "Yee-haw."

And then he yelled, "BAILEY, WHERE ARE YOU?" Bailey came running down the stairs and started jumping all over both Armand and his sister, Grace. We were all so happy to see each other. My sisters were going to be very surprised to see them when they got home from school. I guess Mom and Dad had been planning this surprise for us for a while.

Armand was nine, and Grace was eleven. They were used to dogs, as at home they have a dog named Louie. I think Louie is a little crazy like me. Maybe even a little worse, since he likes to chew things like shoes. I know this because the last time my parents visited Louisville, they came home with a missing flip-flop, and I heard them say that Louie had eaten the other one. Oops! I think Louie is going to attend a doggy-training program soon so he can learn to be a better listener.

I know what it's like to attend school.

I miss those days, Mr. Albert. We had

some good times at school when I was

training, didn't we?

Okay, back to Armand. He couldn't wait

to take Bailey and me out for a walk, so

off we went. Armand asked Grace to

come with us, and she agreed, but she

was *not cleaning up the poop* if we went.

I thought that was funny because *some-*

one has to clean it up, and it sounded like

Grace was not going to touch it. Siblings*

* Siblings are brothers and/or sisters who have the same
parents.

can be so silly toward one another and make each other do things they wouldn't normally do on their own. I get it because Bailey manipulates* me sometimes into doing things I don't always want to do-especially when it comes to getting up on the kitchen table when Mom and Dad are not looking.

As soon as Armand and Grace leashed us up, they pulled us out the door so fast. I could tell they wanted us to get outside quickly. It must have still been cold in Kentucky, and they were excited about

* Manipulate is when you influence change.

the warm Florida weather. Thank goodness it had stopped raining and the sun had come out!

Off we went on our walk. First, we came across the prettiest dog on our circle: Bella. Oh Bella, she has such a sparkle in her eye. I think she likes me. She never really pays much attention to Bailey, just me. Then a few doors down we saw another dog named Daisy. She was outside with her human brother Spencer and sister Jamie. Everyone in the neighborhood thinks Daisy and I look alike. I don't think this is cool because Daisy is a girl dog and a really beautiful one. Okeydokey, so maybe that means I'm handsome, since we look alike?

Daisy is new in our neighborhood. Spencer and Jamie waited a long time for Daisy to be born. Their parents drove them to North Carolina to meet Daisy's mom when she was pregnant, and then a few months later, they drove back to North Carolina and brought Daisy home. Daisy is so, so lucky because her human brother and sister are homeschooled, so she gets to be with them all day while they study. Just a few weeks ago, though, Daisy had to go to the hospital, and it was really scary. I kept walking around the circle every day, hoping to see her, but days went by, and she was not outside. I know what it's like to be sick and kept hoping Daisy didn't have an ongoing sickness like my Addison's disease or my grandmother Lou Lou's Parkinson's disease,* which makes her shake a lot.

Okay, back to my walk, Armand and I kept walking, and I was so glad to be hanging out with him and with Grace, but I

---

* **Parkinson's disease** is a disorder of a person's nervous system that affects movement. Most people with this disease shake a lot.

couldn't stop thinking about Daisy and wondering when I would see her again. Uh-oh! Then I had to poop. Too funny. So who was going to pick up my poop, Armand or Grace? Ten bucks said it would be Grace. When I poop, I always make eye contact with whoever is walking me, so Armand it was. I kept looking at Armand, and I could tell he really didn't want to deal with picking up my poop, even though he had the bag in his hand. Sure enough, as soon as I was done, he stopped looking at me and handed the bag to Grace. They started to argue, and while they were doing that, I decided to bury my poop. Ha-ha! I scraped my hind legs very fast to dig a little hole and put my poop in there. I was having such a great time with this.

Armand turned around and started looking everywhere for my poop and could not find it, and then he started yelling again at Grace to help him find it. Grace looked and looked, and they then decided maybe I didn't really poop, so we headed back to the house. I just wanted to skip home because I thought it was so funny that I fooled them both. I must confess* I learned this little trick of burying my poop from Bella. I've seen her do this a couple of times, and I thought it was so clever.* Bella is so smart and well behaved. Her dad doesn't even use a leash to walk her; she follows right behind him and walks in a straight line with her head held high. Most anytime I walk by her house, she's outside

* **Confess** is when you admit to something.
* **Clever** is when an animal or person is smart about doing something.

lying in her driveway, and when Mom, Dad, and I approach, Bella gracefully gets up, like a princess, and sniffs me and then circles around me.

I look forward to seeing Bella when we go on walks. Y'know, we dogs don't appear to care so much about things on the outside, but, Mr. Albert, as you know, I'm special. I really seem to connect with humans and their feelings. I've learned so much from my family. It's great having sisters and cousins and so many doggy friends on my street. There are just too many to tell you about today. There is

Oreo, Coco, Nessie, Roxy, and others, and even a cat like Martin, the cat you and I lived with. Oh, and there is the cutest bunny that hops around our neighborhood. I see her on our nighttime walks, and I nicknamed her the "Bay Hill Bunny."

Yup, you guessed it—time for a snooze. I'm going to go dream about Daisy coming home soon from the hospital.

Ta-ta for now. Lick, lick, woof, wooof.

LETTER TEN

Dear Mr. Albert,

So I told you that I have a swimming pool. It has a screen around it, and I can see out everywhere, including when I look up. The best part about the screen over the pool is that squirrels run across the top of it, and I can chase them. I just love❤ squirrels. I can be doing anything, but if I see a squirrel, I have to try to get up close to it. I haven't been swimming yet, but I can't wait to go! I keep thinking about running and jumping into the pool, but I'm not sure if I should do that just yet. Plus, every time I think about going into the pool, I see my one special squirrel friend—which, of course, I need to chase after!

Did I mention that my dad started traveling a lot for his job and working less from the house? Yup. I miss having him home every day, but I still get to do nearly everything. The only major difference is my mom and sisters can't walk us every morning all the way around the street that we live on, which is a big circle. This week, though, my mom took me on a walk by myself, just the two of us. It's always special when she does that. I get to sniff around more-, and you know I like sniffing!

I must confess that my squirrel girlfriend, whom BTW, I named Susie, was following us yesterday on our walk. For a split second, I was looking at this ugly duck in the lake, and when I turned around to see if she was still there, Susie was gone! I thought maybe she ran off because I wasn't paying attention to her, but instead, she had run ahead of us. I pulled on my leash and started chasing after her to play. Normally I can't get too close to her because I'm on my patio, and she's on the other side of the screen. So, I can only see her, not touch her. All I could think about was how maybe today, just maybe, we could meet face-to-face, with nothing between us. I could hardly contain my excitement!

Today was turning out a little crazy for my mom, as I ended up walking her instead of letting her walk me! Yes, that's right; I was dragging her down the sidewalk as I barked as loudly as I could, yet in a sweet tone, so as not to scare Susie. Susie was running sort of in a zigzag. All

I could think of is that because we lived in Florida, I was taught by you, Mr. Albert, to run in a zigzag from an alligator, if I was chased. So, did Susie think I was an alligator? Hmm... Oh, then I stopped in my tracks and decided to sit upright and look as handsome as I possibly could, hoping I would catch her attention. By golly, it worked! Susie stopped in her tracks, turned around, and stared at me.

Now, one of my fave things, as you know, Mr. Albert, is a good staring contest. I wondered how patient my mom would be with this staring contest. Mom ended up being super patient. I think she was anxious to see what was going to happen as she pulled me close to her and held my leash a little extra tight. "*I won, I won!*" Susie actually ended up looking down and started running in a zigzag again, but this time toward me! I think she wanted to give me a big hug or maybe even a little kiss on my cheek. She must have been running one hundred miles an hour, and before I knew it, I was holding Susie in my mouth. Yes! I had her *in my mouth!* I wasn't hurting her; I was just holding her, as I wanted to see her up close and get to know her.

You can only imagine how my mom started to scream, saying, "Prince, put her down at once!" So, I did, and Susie skipped away, looking back at me a couple of times while smiling. Mom then rushed me back to the house, rinsed my mouth out, and seemed really, really... nervous. She then picked up the phone, and I heard her speaking with my doctor. She was asking about something called rabies.* Next thing I knew, I was in the car, and I could tell we were headed straight to the place where I see my doctor.

* **Rabies** is a contagious and possibly fatal viral disease that is spread after an animal bite.

Usually when we get there, I have to wait patiently in the lobby, but this time they put me right into a room, and the doctor came in immediately. Frankly, I've never seen my mom this worried about me. The doctor looked me over and left the room to discuss something outside the door without us. I'm not really sure what she was doing or saying or to whom she was speaking. When she came back in, she said to my mom that it was possible I could have rabies (even though I had been vaccinated*) and that I needed to either

* **Vaccinate** is to give an animal or person a shot to help prevent them from getting sick.

stay at the hospital for observation* or I could go home. If I went home, I would have to stay in my crate for days, and my mom would need to keep a close eye on me to see how I was feeling.

From what I understood, rabies was a really bad, contagious virus. My heart was beating so fast that I could feel it in my head. I started whimpering and almost crying. *Doggone it, what have I done?* I thought. *I can't believe Susie could have a virus that made me sick. This can't be!* My mom called my dad because he was

* Observation is a careful look at someone or something.

out of town and asked for his advice. My dad said something about wanting to research it and asked if he could call her back in a few minutes. In the meantime, the doctor came back in and asked if a decision had been made. My mom's voice was shaky because she really had no idea what would be best for me.

She was very upset, and all I wanted to do was tell her how sorry I was. I'm sure she could see it in my droopy eyes. Thank goodness her cell phone started ringing; my dad was calling back. I could hear my dad telling Mom to call Ms. Becky and get her opinion. I actually thought that was a great idea, since Ms. Becky cared so much about me and had a lot of experience taking care of dogs. Sure enough, my mom called Ms. Becky, but the phone rang and rang; she must not have been home. The doctor was back in our room, waiting for my mom to give her a decision whether I was going to stay at the hospital or go home. I was so nervous that I was actually shaking. My mom finally made the decision that I would go home and that she would keep a close eye on me. She assured the doctor

I would be kept in my crate and away from my brother, Bailey.

We got back into the car, and I put my head down on the seat. I was so sad. *What have I done?* As soon as we got home, my mom took me potty real quick, and then she took me right upstairs into her bedroom and straight into my crate. The next morning, she took me out as usual, but instead of eating in the kitchen with Bailey, I had to eat in my crate, and I couldn't play or do anything. My mom stayed in her bed, next to my crate, all day. I could see she was doing some kind of research on her laptop about rabies as she dozed on and off, like she does nearly every day. My mom's illness makes her very tired, and some days she swells badly. Today was one of those days she had to take a shot, and I was worried about her, because I could see she was stressed about me. Oh dear, Mr. Albert, *what have I done?* I hope this turns out okay; I'll let you know.

Ta-ta and night-night for now. Your VERY... sad Prince.

LETTER ELEVEN

Dear Mr. Albert,

The next morning, Mom took me out on my morning walk. We went a little later than our usual time because she didn't want me to be in contact with any of my other animal or human friends. She carefully took me all the way down our street and back. Just like we normally do. I was so happy she did, because I was afraid she might not ever do it again after my bad behavior. Thank goodness none of my friends were out that day. Not even Susie was around.

That same morning, Mom ended up calling this place called Animal Control. She asked them about squirrels and whether or not they typically could get rabies. She went on to explain everything that had happened between Susie and me. She talked about how I ended up hugging Susie by holding her in my mouth. The nice lady at Animal Control explained to my mom that there has rarely been a report of a squirrel having rabies. Plus, squirrels are so fast, with 180-degree vision, that the chances of them being caught and bitten by another animal that has rabies are very slim.

When I heard this, I started running in circles in my crate. I just knew at that moment I was going to be okay. Everyone was worried that because Susie had allowed me to get close to her that she was sick with this virus. Nope, this was not the case. Yeah...! I'm so, so happy that she and I are both just... fine. Thank goodness we can still be BFF's (best friends forever). It was love❤ at first sight for Susie and me!

My mom thanked the lady, hung up the phone, and quickly opened my crate to let me out to play with Bailey and all of my toys. Woo-hoo... free at last! Yippee! After reuniting with Bailey and playing for a few minutes, I rushed down the stairs and out my doggy door to look for Susie. I barked and barked as loudly as I could from one side of the patio all the way to the other side. Finally, I saw her and a couple of her friends run over the top of the screen.

We played hide-and-go-seek for a long time, and before I went inside, I put my paw on the screen from the inside, and Susie put her foot up on the screen, from the outside. Our brown eyes stared at one another. I gave a friendly little

bark, she made a little squeaky noise, and we both went our separate ways.

Honestly, Mr. Albert, I'm just not sure if I ever want to see her again without the screen between us. I guess we'll just have to wait and see what happens. I just don't want anything to happen to her. I'll keep you posted, though; I promise.

Ta-ta for now. Lick, lick, woof, wooof.

LETTER TWELVE

Dear Mr. Albert,

Today I realized that sometimes I do things that my mom thinks are really great. So yeah, you guessed it—I end up getting a bone or an EXTRA TREAT. *Woo-hoo for me!* I figured out a few weeks ago that Mom is always looking for her reading glasses, which she has many pairs of, all over the house. One day she was looking for a pair, and I knew exactly where they were, so I got them and brought them to her. She was so, so excited about it; she kept thanking me and saying, "Good job, Prince!" And she gave me a bone. Yeah, yeah, so I figured out that by bringing her things, like her glasses, I can easily get a bone or treat. Love❤ ... it! Heehee.... LOL.

Well, later that night was interesting. Mom, Dad, Bailey, and I were watching a movie. I was begging Paris to rub my belly because she always knows the right place to scratch. She was not paying any attention to me, since she was too involved with her movie. So to get her attention, I thought I would bring Paris her fave pair of sunglasses. The glasses thing seemed to work to get Mom's attention, so I thought it would work with Paris, too.

I jumped off the couch and ran straight to her room and opened the drawer where she keeps her sunglasses. I picked up the bright-yellow sunglasses that her BFF had given her, and I ran back into the living room where she was. The sunglasses caught her eye immediately, and she started yelling at me.

Uh-oh! I could tell she was *not* happy. Why

was she yelling at me? *Yikes,* I thought. I

haven't done anything wrong. What the

heck? I just wanted a belly rub (oh and

maybe a bone, heehee...). Paris thought I

was trying to destroy her sunglasses,

so she made me apologize to Mom and Dad for disrupting* their movie, and then she made me bring the yellow sunglasses back to her room where I had found them. No bone for me. *Bummer.* Well, I tried. I felt bad, but I love❤ finding things to bring back to them. I always drop whatever it is in front of them and say, "Ta-da!" And my mom usually says, "Oh no, Prince, now what?"

Okeydokey, I'm going to go ring my bells on the front door, where my parents

---

* **Disrupting** is causing someone (or something) to *stop* what he or she is doing.

hung some chimes that sound like bells when I touch them. This really helps me tell my family when I want to go potty. Ms. Becky taught them to do that for me.

Ta-ta for now. Lick, lick, and woof, wooof.

LETTER THIRTEEN

Dear Mr. Albert,

Since living with my new family, I've felt more like a human than ever before. Mom, Dad, and my sisters talk to me all the time, just like they talk to each other. Sometimes, though, it seems like they're talking to me like I'm a baby, but I don't really mind it. As I've mentioned, I don't always pay attention very well, so they have to repeat themselves several times before I get it. But recently,

I decided I would start trying a little harder. After all, I have the coolest family ever. Not only do I want to listen better, so I can take everything in, but I've decided that for a dog, I'm a lot like a human.

As you know, I still have Addison's disease, and I heard my doctor say girls and boys of all ages can have this disease. I'm also starting to realize how my mom is feeling every day. If she's not having a good day, I can communicate to her that she needs to take her medication. I put my head on her chest and give her a certain look, and then she knows she probably needs her shot.

See, I'm so much like a human, and I feel needed, since I help Mom. I've even tried to learn to speak like humans. My vocal cords don't always allow me to pronounce words right, so I just end up making silly sounds, but I try. One of my fave sounds is A-R-G-H (kinda like a pirate), and I say it very high pitched. It's very catchy.

It's summer now and really hot outside. My sisters are going to sleepaway camp in Wisconsin, and I won't see them for six weeks or more. They promised to send me a postcard. I plan to check the mailbox every single day. I'll miss them so much.

Paris keeps counting down the days until she gets to go back to her camp. Some kids get homesick when they go to sleep-away camp and don't see their parents, *but not Paris!* She gets "camp-sick" during the school year! No, no, she's not really sick... that's just a saying. It really means she misses camp and wants to go back.

Both my sisters are like me and very into sports. So going to camp is great for them. They waterski, hike, play tennis, and much more. Thank goodness they like to play sports because they know how important it is to me to play with my tennis ball every day. They love♥ that I can

catch it in midair every time they throw it

to me. I never miss! I'm headed to find my

ball right now!

Ta-ta for now. Lick, lick, and woof,

wooof.

LETTER FOURTEEN

Dear Mr. Albert,

My parents and sisters always speak so much about how we should appreciate what we have in our lives. I do. I really do. I know when I was at the prison and you were teaching me to help disabled veterans, I really appreciated everything you did to help me. I was sad when I learned I could no longer be assigned to someone disabled. I was really looking forward to sharing everything I learned with someone who needed my services. Phooey. But seriously, I know I can still leave a legacy.* After all, my family has continued to teach me well. *Can I share a secret with you, Mr. Albert?* Many nights I dream of being a superhero dog with a cape and Bailey as my sidekick!

* A **legacy** is what an animal or person is known for after he or she has died. His or her ideas are passed on to future generations.

I often run around the house and jump from one thing to another, pretending I'm a super-hero. I know I don't have superpowers, but I'll never forget how brave I had to be when I was sick and alone at the hospital.

So I'll always continue to be brave! Mr. Albert, I'm very grateful to have found a beautiful house to live in. I hope you're happy for me.

BTW, I saw Daisy today. She came home from the hospital. I bet she was brave, too. Her doctor told her she has to be careful about playing too much out-side (like me) but that the medicine she will take forever (like me) will keep her healthy. Thank goodness.

I'm so thankful for my animal friends and of course, my doggy brother, Bailey, and my new forever human family. Not a day goes by that I'm not entertained and reminded how much I'm loved♥. I'm blessed to have been adopted by my family. Until next time, Mr. Albert, one final *big slobbery*... lick, lick and woof, wooof.

I'll always *love♥ you*, Mr. Albert, *now and forever*.

The end (for now).

"Prince's Fave *BIG WORDS* Glossary"

1. **Addison's disease (ad·di·son's dis·ease)**: A rare condition that causes the body to not make enough hormones to keep itself working properly.

2. **Adrenal glands (ad·re·nal glands)**: Located on top of each kidney in both animals and humans. If glands in our bodies are working properly, they help keep us healthy.

3. **Affectionate (af·fec·tion·ate)**: Showing warmth and kindness to someone or something that you really like or love❤. Affection is communicated by words, gestures, or touches.

4. **Apprehensive (ap·pre·hen·sive)**: When you feel uneasy or scared causing nervousness.

5. **Authentic (au·then·tic)**: Something that's real; it's not fake or pretend.

6. **Celebrity (ce·leb·ri·ty)**: An animal or person who is famous or very well known.

7. **Citizen (cit·i·zen)**: A person who lives in a particular place or country.

8. **Clever (clev·er):** When an animal or person is smart about doing something.

9. **Complimentary (com·pli·men·ta·ry):** An expression used when explaining you liked what someone did.

10. **Confess (con·fess):** When you admit to something.

11. **Confidence (con·fi·dence):** A feeling of pride and of being certain of yourself or your actions.

12. **Crisis (cri·sis):** A difficult or dangerous situation that needs serious attention.

13. **Cruelty (cru·el·ty):** When an animal or person is treated very badly.

14. **Disabled (dis·a·bled):** When someone is affected by an illness or injury. Some disabilities can be clear to see, such as when someone must use a wheelchair. But disabilities in people or animals may not always be visible.

15. **Discombobulated (dis·com·bob·u·lat·ed):** When things are mixed up, not in order, confusing.

16. **Disrupting (dis·rupt·ing):** Causing someone (or something) to *stop* what he or she is doing.

17. **Enthusiastic (en·thu·si·as·tic)**: When you feel excited and very interested in something.

18. **Foster home (fos·ter home)**: Is a temporary place for animals or children to live while being cared for by people or a family who have volunteered to take care of them.

19. **Gluten-free (glu·ten free)**: A special diet in which wheat and grains, including barley, rye, oat, and more are not eaten.

20. **Grateful (grate·ful)**: A feeling of being thankful.

21. **Homeless (home·less)**: When an animal or person has no place to live and therefore often ends up living on the streets.

22. **Hormones (hor·mones)**: Are chemicals in animal and human blood that control certain cell and organ functions.

23. **Inmates (in·mates)**: People who live in jail or a correctional facility because they broke the law. They are separated from family and friends.

24. **Intimidating (in·tim·i·dat·ing)**: Something that makes you frightened or scared.

25. **Legacy (leg·a·cy)**: What an animal or person is known for after he or she has died. His or her ideas are passed on to future generations.

26. **Manipulate (ma·nip·u·late)**: When you influence change.

27. **Nonchalant (non·cha·lant)**: Relaxed or calm in a way that shows you're not worried about anything.

28. **Observation (ob·ser·va·tion)**: A careful look at someone or something.

29. **Overwhelmed (o·ver·whelmed)**: When an animal or person has too many emotions. This can be a positive or negative feeling.

30. **Parkinson's disease (par·kin·son's dis·ease)**: A disorder of a person's nervous system that affects movement. Most people with this disease shake a lot.

31. **Prison (pris·on)**: A place where people who have broken the law must live to make up for the bad thing(s) they have done. People who go to prison may have to stay for months, years, or even a lifetime. Prison is also called a jail or a correctional facility.

32. **Rabies (ra·bies)**: A contagious and possibly fatal viral disease that is spread after an animal bite.

33. **Siblings (sib·lings)**: Brothers and/or sisters who have the same parents.

34. **Soup kitchen (soup kit·chen)**: A place where food (such as soup and bread) is given to poor people.

35. **Unconditionally (un·con·di·tion·al·ly)**: When you love❤ someone or something no matter what.

36. **Vaccinate (vac·ci·nate)**: Is to give an animal or person a shot to help prevent them from getting sick.

37. **Veteran (vet·er·an)**: A person who served as a member of the armed forces and is now retired. Veterans protected our country and are highly respected for their service.

38. **Veterinarian (vet·er·i·nar·i·an)**: A doctor who takes care of animals.

39. **Wisdom (wis·dom)**: Knowledge gained from life experiences and learning from them.

"Prince's Fave Abbreviations"

1. **BFF:** Best friends forever
2. **BTW**: By the way
3. **FAVE**: Favorite
4. **FOMO**: Fear of missing out
5. **HAK**: Hugs and kisses
6. **ILY**: I love❤ you
7. **JK**: Just kidding
8. **LMK**: Let me know
9. **LOL**: Laughing out loud
10. **NP**: No problem
11. **OMG**: Oh my goodness
12. **OMW**: On my way
13. **TBH**: To be honest
14. **THX**: Thanks
15. **TTYL**: Talk to you later

Mr. Albert, when I learned from you in the Dogs 4 Disabled Veterans B.A.R.K. Program, you taught me over one hundred commands and tasks. The doctor told me to not work on all of them, since I have Addison's disease. Ah—but you can ask anyone who knows me, and they will tell you "Prince's Fave Commands" still are:

Back up

Closer

Come

Crate

Down

Drop it

Ears

Eyes

Forward

Head down

Heel

Help

Hug

Hurry up

Kisses

Leash

Leave it

Lights off

Lights on

Mouth

No bark

Open

Paw(s)— right paw/left paw

Paws up

Phone

Pick it up

Puppy pill

Roll-over

Sit

Sleep

Stay

Teeth

Time out

Turn left

Turn right

Work

Some new commands I've learned from my family include
the following:

Ball
Bed
Door
Car
Get it
Move
Stop
Toy

And they still say my name before every command.
Like "Prince Sit."

A *shout-out* to Dr. Rachel Schwartz for taking the *best* care of Prince and to the Shaggy Dog pet salon for keeping him looking spiffy! Prince wouldn't look and feel as good as he does without you all!

Love. ❤ Live. ❤ Bark.

"Prince's Fave Joke"

Question:
Why did the tree think Prince was talking to it?

Answer:
Because Prince kept saying, "Bark, bark, bark!"
　　…Ha-ha!

"Prince's Fave T-shirt Says"

Prince lives happily and adventurously
with his two sisters, parents,
and older doggy brother, Bailey.

Oh, here is a note from my sisters Sage and Paris: You're really going to love❤ Prince and can write him a letter yourself. He might even answer you!

Here is his website: **www.princethedog.com**

89756913R00085

Made in the USA
Columbia, SC
20 February 2018

OPPORTU

OPPORTUNITIES

in

Culinary
Careers

REVISED EDITION

MARY DONOVAN

VGM Career Books

Chicago New York San Francisco Lisbon London Madrid Mexico City
Milan New Delhi San Juan Seoul Singapore Sydney Toronto

Library of Congress Cataloging-in-Publication Data

Donovan, Mary Deirdre, 1955–
      Opportunities in culinary careers / Mary Donovan. — Rev. ed.
         p.   cm. — (VGM opportunities series)
      Includes bibliographical references.
      ISBN 0-07-141148-8
      1. Food service—Vocational guidance.   I. Title.   II. Series.

TX911.3.V62D66   2003
647.95'023—dc21   2003050167

  2 3 4 5 6 7 8 9 0 LBM/LBM 2 1 0 9 8 7 6 5 4

ISBN 0-07-141148-8

Interior design by Rattray Design

McGraw-Hill books are available at special quantity discounts to use as premiums and sales promotions, or for use in corporate training programs. For more information, please write to the Director of Special Sales, Professional Publishing, McGraw-Hill, Two Penn Plaza, New York, NY 10121-2298. Or contact your local bookstore.

This book is printed on acid-free paper.

CONTENTS

v

FOREWORD

THERE HAS NEVER been a better time to begin a career in the culinary arts. Job openings for chefs, cooks, and other kitchen workers are expected to be plentiful throughout the decade. The variety of possible careers offers something for anyone who is interested in this field, from the private chef at an exclusive restaurant to the manager of food services at a hospital or university. People with all tastes and talents can find the perfect job within the scope of the culinary arts.

A career in the culinary field demands dedication, education, hard work, and talent. Even an established chef must constantly study, travel, and experiment with new foods and new methods of cooking traditional dishes. The hours may be long and the demands taxing, but the potential rewards, in terms of both salary and personal satisfaction, are great.

Many current trends indicate the continued importance of the culinary arts. Increased leisure time, interest in various ethnic cuisines, and the demand for healthier food options present interesting opportunities and challenges for today's chefs. Institutional settings offer another, often overlooked, area where chefs can excel, and the public is increasingly coming to expect high quality, nutritious foods in these settings.

The culinary arts are a rewarding and highly respected career choice. Fine cuisine, once the exclusive privilege of the ruling elite, is now available to greater and greater numbers of people. Those who prepare fine food will find many and varied opportunities for success in their careers.

The Editors
VGM Career Books

PREFACE

THE CULINARY ARTS have to do primarily with the preparation of food. There are practically limitless variations on this basic theme. Some of these options may not seem, at first glance, to have very much to do with the typical restaurant environment. However, the food service industry, including the workers that make it click, is large enough to support all of these varied activities.

As you read through this book, you will see that the opportunities you find appealing may well be the traditional roles of cook, baker, chef, food and beverage manager, or owner of a restaurant or hotel. It also will be apparent that there are countless other directions to take. You do have the ability to create your own position. If you have an idea and are willing to work at making it happen, you can succeed.

There are many reasons to join the ranks of those who work with food for a living. For most people in the culinary arts, the most important are a basic love for food and cooking and a basic desire to make people happy.

The other reasons that may motivate you can be extremely varied, and as you go through your career you will find that what you can offer this industry and what you expect to get back from it will change. This is the stuff that careers are made of. Don't let yourself become stagnant in the same dull routine. It is important that you keep your interest alive and your love for food and cooking fresh by trying new foods, new restaurants, new wines, perhaps even new types of work.

Remember the spark that first urged you toward this work, and do your best to nurture it, feed it, and keep it alive and growing. The rewards from this industry are among the greatest you could ever hope to achieve.

1

WHY CHOOSE A CULINARY CAREER?

NEVER BEFORE HAVE so many people been poised to enter the culinary field. It seems that everywhere you turn, you can find stories that at least initially seem to defy logic. A judge resigns her seat and dons chef's whites. A lawyer leaves "the City," moves to Vermont, and opens an inn. And it isn't just those who want to cook, manage a dining room, or run a restaurant who are joining the swelling ranks of this profession.

A Wide-Open Career Path

This field is open to nearly anyone, as long as he or she has a passion for food, a taste for excellence in service and quality, and the energy and spirit that are required to pursue a dream. More women and minorities are finding a respected place in the food service industry. There are career tracks for those with a strong corporate background as well as for those more free-spirited entrepreneurs.

It would be hard to describe the "typical" chef. In fact, many have taken to using the term *culinarian* to describe the broad scope of jobs this industry now encompasses. And the pool of talented professionals clearly demonstrates that there are plenty of exciting, rewarding, and challenging jobs where you can put your personal strengths to use.

You'll find some people who are detail-driven and precise and others who are creative problem solvers. Some are great with numbers. Others have a way with people. There is plenty of work for the scientifically minded and those with a bent for research. People work in for-profit businesses as well as for nonprofits. There are individually owned enterprises and international corporations.

Women are rising to the top of the ladder in ever-increasing numbers. There are many restaurants owned and operated by women. There are many more women executive chefs than ever before. And occupations such as food writing, food photography, and catering seem to offer the challenges and rewards needed for a stimulating career.

How well suited is this industry to accommodating the special concerns of those with families? Workers of both genders are increasingly likely to state that family concerns—day care, time off to care for their families during periods of illness, work hours that encourage "family time" in the evenings and on holidays—are high on their list of priorities.

For those committed to finding or providing family-friendly environments, there are solutions to be found. Work hours do vary widely. Bakers and pastry chefs, for instance, often work from the very early hours until just after lunch. Caterers can often control their working hours to establish a schedule that leaves weekdays free for family. Split shifts and shared jobs are all increasingly available, if you are willing to ask.

Others find that the traditional workplace, be it a restaurant, a gourmet shop, or a bakeshop, simply doesn't have enough flexibility. Instead of trying to shoehorn their "square" lifestyle into a "round" job situation, they are simply breaking out on their own, starting up small businesses and enterprises that help fulfill their culinary aspirations without having to depend upon a system that won't give them enough support to manage their lives and families with comfort.

Minorities in the Culinary Field

In the past, racial prejudice has played a role in consigning many minorities to the kitchen to perform the more menial tasks. Consequently, it has been difficult to move from the nether world of the culinary arts into the limelight as a result of this prejudice. Fortunately, this is changing. One need only look at renowned chefs such as Chef Jimmy Lee, executive chef of the United States Senate, and Chef Rafail Palomino, owner and executive chef of Vida in Manhattan, to realize that racial barriers have begun to crumble.

Due to an ever-growing fascination with cuisines from around the world, there is a corresponding growth in the opportunities for cooks and chefs with a strong grounding in a specific cuisine. The ability to work with ingredients unfamiliar to those trained in classical cuisine and to get the most from equipment that is equally unfamiliar has opened greater opportunities for members of those ethnic communities in today's kitchens.

There is no room in an industry that will go begging for skilled workers in the years to come to let selective blindness keep a valuable source of workers excluded from its ranks.

Physically Challenged People in the Culinary Field

When the notion of a blind chef or a chef who is hard of hearing or who sits in a wheelchair or wears leg braces is first mentioned, many people automatically react with disbelief. But as kitchen equipment and kitchen designs come of age, these physical challenges can certainly be overcome. And as this industry changes to meet the needs of a contemporary society, the type of work required changes as well.

Learning to compensate for certain physical challenges is an individual responsibility, but gaining access to a forum where your talents can shine is everyone's right.

Second (or Third) Career

Many more people find that they change careers at least once during their working lives; others change more often. A great number of those entering the food service industry are making just such a career change. For some this may be a radical change from the type of work they did in their "previous" lives. It is not at all unusual to find someone who once earned his or her living as an accountant, teacher, or librarian turning to the culinary arts. Victims of downsizing or of the Internet bust have also joined the growing ranks of those who turn to the culinary world when job leads in one or another industry start to turn cold.

Life experience counts for a great deal. The more you know about yourself before you enter this field, the surer you can be that you will find your way. You may have found yourself constantly fascinated and intrigued with food and cooking, reading cookbooks and magazines voraciously, and looking for chances to cook new and different dishes for family and friends. You may have found yourself wondering what it would be like to work in a restaurant.

For people such as yourself, it is a good idea to take an entry-level position and test the waters. This is a career different from those you might have known before. The hierarchy depends not upon degrees or published papers. Instead it is the steady practice of the craft, the application of the technique, and the refinement of palate that make the difference.

The culinary arts are demanding and exacting. You will make your way or not depending upon how well you can translate a love of people and food from an abstract idea directly into your work. Freshness of approach and responsiveness to the needs of the paying guest are of the utmost importance.

You may find that the pressures and hours of working in a kitchen are not suited to your lifestyle, or that the adjustments might be too disruptive after years spent at a nine-to-five desk job. Nonetheless, you may still find ways to turn your ambition to work with food into a lucrative and rewarding career.

Room to Grow

Is there still room in this burgeoning field for you? Absolutely! When this book went to press, the National Restaurant Association estimated that in the years ahead there would be a need for some two million skilled and trained workers in the culinary field.

Many will work in hotels and restaurants. But a great many will find new and exciting niches that may not have existed fifteen, ten, or even five years ago. There are plenty of ways to find a good direction in this field. The quick overview that follows should be just a jumping-off point.

Designing and Manufacturing Equipment, Tools, and Other Supplies

Even though you might think that all the new and exciting equipment you could ever need has already been developed, there is a constant drive to produce new tools, new ways to perform labor-intensive or tedious jobs, or better-quality versions of tools we already use.

Technology and the Chef

Of all the new pieces of equipment, tools, and gadgets coming into use in the modern kitchen, the tool with the greatest potential is probably the computer. Today the uses for computers have gone well beyond inventory and costing applications. Many development and design, staffing, budgeting, forecasting, and other tasks can be done readily with it. The Internet is opening the doors even further; some might say that the Internet and the Web have blown the doors off.

Distance learning and modules in areas such as server training, sexual harassment, and sanitation certification can be implemented readily through the use of a variety of software and interactive applications. CD-ROMs with quick or real-time videos are important training tools. And, of course, online access to libraries, chat rooms, websites, and other resources have improved and changed forever the way that food service establishments operate.

As the nutritional concerns of people in both the United States and Canada continue to change the ways that chefs are preparing and presenting foods, computers have another important role to play. There is no longer any doubt that nutritional cooking is here to stay. Indeed, almost a whole industry has grown up around the fact that baby boomers are still looking for ways to enjoy life without threatening or compromising their health.

The specific software applications available to the chef and the nutritionist today make it relatively easy to analyze recipes, though there is some skill involved to do this. It is important to understand how cooking affects foods and changes the overall nutritional content of a dish in ways that are not immediately obvious. For instance, a marinade does not necessarily get absorbed 100 percent by meat, so you have to scale back the values for the marinade, make sure that you select the correct cooking method, and assign the appropriate portion size.

Software and online applications for the kitchen are still emerging. The tried-and-true systems for costing, recipe management, and customer database information are being revised and released constantly, so keep your eyes open to find the software that is best—or unearth a special niche for yourself as a developer and designer of software.

Developing Learning Tools for Students

According to the myth and lore of nostalgic cooking magazines, there was a time when we all learned to cook and love food by working with our mothers and grandmothers in their kitchens, as well as when we gathered around the family table for dinner. If there is any doubt, we can all rest assured that those golden days are gone.

Culinary students, including home cooks, need plenty of information if they are to succeed. Books and radio and television programs; demonstrations; and working in schools dedicated to food service are some of the areas in which a person with a penchant for teaching can find a role in this industry.

You might work on videos or programs that can demonstrate a new cooking technique or explain the proper preparation and presentation of a dish developed for a chain of restaurants. These programs require more than simply a stove and someone behind a camcorder. They also demand a scriptwriter knowledgeable enough about food to make the information accessible and valuable.

You might work on books, learning programs, textbooks, or lectures. These products need to be developed by someone with a strong culinary background if they are to be useful for the intended student.

Advertising and Promotion

Restaurants, hotels, chains, and distributors all need to get the word out to the public that they are there. The growth of advertising and public relations firms that deal exclusively with food is a recent phenomenon, but it is one that clearly indicates the importance and economic value of the culinary arts. Agencies that provide the advertising needed for an operation demand workers who are skilled enough in the culinary arts to make sure that the right kind of message is getting out to the right market.

Summary

As you can see, the range of opportunities, from working with your hands to working with computers, is vast. The culinary arts need virtually every available worker, so the old prejudices are dying out at an ever-increasing rate.

Women, minorities, and workers who are physically challenged—all of these people who might previously have found it difficult to enter the professional kitchen—are finding themselves going to the very top of their careers and enjoying the respect of their peers. These changes will continue, and their good effects are being felt everywhere.

The culinary arts can be learned, even if you have already started in another career. And very often, the skills that you might have applied to a different line of work can be made to benefit not only you, but the entire cooking industry as well.

Everyone has a story about how and when they decided to look into a career in the culinary arts. Your experience will certainly be unique, just as you are. But once you have made the decision, you will find that this is an industry that feeds the soul, the mind, *and* the body.

2

A NOBLE PROFESSION

ONCE HUMAN BEINGS learned to tame fire for their own use, it was not long before they realized that not only did fire provide light and heat, it also could change how food tasted. Of course, there is no exact answer as to how long it took for people to begin the process of learning to cook, but we can speculate what course that evolution might have taken.

Over time, people learned to raise a variety of foods, including grains. Animals were domesticated and raised as well. The next logical step was to produce a variety of pots, racks, and other cooking utensils to handle these foods. First, pouches of skin might have been used to hold water so that grains could be boiled. Eventually, pots of clay, and then of metal, made it a much simpler matter to boil meats, vegetables, and grains.

Some of the advances made—learning to make leavened breads and cheeses and discovering the variety of foods that could and could not be eaten—are so important that it is almost impossible to imagine what would happen if the accumulated knowledge of thousands and thousands of years should be lost overnight. One wonders what the reaction of the first person to taste cheese or beer might have been, and where the courage to try something so foreign to the tongue came from.

The history of cooking is linked to the history of civilization. Although we may not have exact records of who first learned to harvest rice and boil it, or who first sampled an oyster, we can be certain that as soon as groups of people gathered into communities, there was cooking going on.

In earlier times, and even today in countries where most people live in villages, communal cooking activities including bread-, sausage-, and cheese-making helped keep the community alive. Everyone did his or her share, and they did it together.

Today, in a society where every home has a refrigerator, a stove, and usually a microwave, it is sometimes difficult to remember that cooking has always been, even from the rudest beginnings of society, a noble and necessary profession.

These days, when the culinary arts come under discussion, the picture that first comes to mind is a restaurant chef dressed in a white jacket, checkered pants, and wearing a *toque blanche*—the tall, pleated, white chef's hat. There is a tradition of excellence, an aura of authority surrounding anyone rightly referred to as "chef."

Unlike many European nations such as France, Italy, and Switzerland, the United States has not been noted for its chefs. For a number of reasons, there was a feeling that working as a chef was not as respectable as working in a "real profession," such as teaching, law, or medicine.

Many people used to consider working in the food service industry as synonymous with being someone's servant. Since only the wealthy had servants, our democratic nation has fostered the notion that we are all masters, and that no one who holds himself or herself in high esteem would willingly work at the beck and call of another.

Since the last world war, however, this attitude in our society has gradually changed. From that time on, the idea of culinary arts as a career has taken on new respect in the eyes of society, and more importantly, in the eyes of those who have decided to make cooking their livelihood. Chefs, caterers, pastry chefs, and others who work in the culinary arts are coming into the limelight. Today, the chef is often as much a glamorous superstar as an actor might be.

At the same time that this increase in respectability was beginning, Americans were becoming increasingly sophisticated about the kinds of foods they enjoyed eating. People, who in the normal course of their lives, would never have gone to Italy, France, or the Pacific Islands, found themselves eating and enjoying strange new foods. Because of this new awareness of the pleasures of food, an increase of disposable income in the years following World War II, and a simultaneous increase in the amount of time spent away from the home as the two-income family has become the norm, the inevitable has occurred. More people are eating more meals away from their homes with every passing year.

These changes have been gradual, and it is not easy to pinpoint the exact moment that they began to occur in this country. In Europe and most Asian countries, the position of chef is a revered one. It is arrived at only after years of training and dedication. Aspiring to excel in the culinary arts for these societies is a commendable path.

The United States has taken some time to arrive at that same belief, and the change is not yet complete. But before we go any deeper into a discussion of the culinary arts as a career, let's take a look at how this field has grown and changed over the course of time.

The Culinary Field Through the Ages

Throughout history there have been numerous examples of the power and prestige associated with the position of "chef." As societies gradually became advanced enough to establish a formal power structure, the leading families would very often demonstrate their wealth and power by employing the best chefs. In some cases, a chef could be a prize brought back from a war to serve the household.

Louis XIV had a contingent of more than five hundred people whose sole function was to attend to the meals of the king and of the rest of the court. Members of the nobility, who paid for the privilege of serving the king, held these positions.

The First Restaurant

As the feudal system began to break down and a more democratic society with a middle class began to evolve, the chef's role changed. And an event that happened in 1765 played a pivotal role in deciding what the new profile of a chef's job would become.

The owner of a café in Paris, who is known today only by the name Boulanger, won a historic court case against the caterers' guild. Until this time, a café owner such as Monsieur Boulanger was entitled to serve his guests only drinks and "restorative broths." Any prepared foods served hot would have to come from the caterer. When Boulanger chose to offer his guests a dish of sheep's feet stewed in a white sauce, he was taken to court by the guild of caterers. The court did not consider this dish a stew and ruled that he had not violated the law. As time passed, this first "restaurateur" continued to expand his menu.

For the first time, guests could have a meal somewhere other than at an inn or from a caterer. And for the first time, the fine cuisine that was previously the exclusive privilege of the elite was available to greater and greater numbers of people.

The Birth of the Brigade System

Auguste Escoffier and Cesar Ritz were directly responsible for making the restaurant a suitable and even desirable place in which men and women alike could dine and be seen. By the time that the Savoy Hotel in London became an acceptable part of life, it had changed forever the way in which the public viewed restaurants. No longer simply stopping places for weary travelers, or clubs for men, restaurants had started on the way to becoming the institutions they are today.

In the United States, we have been a little slower than European countries to use restaurants and hotels as not only a place to eat, but also a place to meet, conduct business, entertain family and friends, and, in general, celebrate life. But as lifestyles in America have changed in inevitable response to the increasing demands upon free time, people find more and more that they do not have the time to entertain in their own homes by themselves. Nor do they find it possible to retain a personal staff to take care of the domestic chores that such entertaining would automatically require.

Enter the restaurant. Restaurants have evolved from a *table d'hôte* in which the guest simply paid for the meal that was offered. At that time, there was no choice involved. The word *restaurant* today, however, conjures up images of a menu with a wide number of selections, each one with a separate price. The guest makes a selection from the menu for each course. The term *a la carte restaurant* reflects this: *a la carte* translates from the French as "from the menu."

Kitchen Organization and Positions

The staff in a kitchen needs to be able to prepare, at any given moment, a wide number of items. The size of the kitchen staff can range from one person to a large group, classically known as the *brigade*. The size of the kitchen staff is determined equally by the number of meals the restaurant commonly serves and how extensive the menu is.

The number of people actually employed in a kitchen will vary greatly from one operation to the next. The organization detailed here is suitable for a very large operation, such as a hotel. In most circumstances the responsibilities of any given position may be changed to accommodate a smaller staff.

Executive Positions

The main responsibility of providing food that is delicious, creative, and of excellent quality falls to this first line of chefs in the kitchen, which include the master chef, executive chef, head chef, and sous-chef.

Master Chef

This is the highest accolade the American Culinary Federation can bestow on a chef. It is achieved only after having met stringent requirements for experience, education, and competition. The candidate must do a great deal of study and preparation for the grueling exam administered by other chefs, most of them master chefs as well.

The candidate must demonstrate skill of an exceptional level in a number of different competencies, including cooking, baking, presentation, cold foods, nutrition, and facility design. Above all, however, the chef must demonstrate the ability to perform at consistently high levels under what are some of the most difficult of circumstances.

Executive Chef

The executive chef is in charge of large kitchens, even chains of kitchens. This title is not capriciously applied; to truly deserve this title, the chef must have either a diploma or a certificate from a school or organization recognized as having the authority to grant the title. The initials "C.E.C." following a chef's name indicate "Certified Executive Chef," which means that certain basic standards for education and experience have been met. Although there are some relatively young C.E.C.s, they all must have fulfilled the same criteria.

The responsibilities of this position are varied. The chef oversees the operation of the entire kitchen, and he or she is ultimately responsible for the food and the service offered by an establishment. To this person falls the responsibility for developing and maintaining the standards of preparation and service of food, in accordance with the practices of the company or facility. The executive chef develops menus and, where necessary and appropriate, develops and tests recipes to ensure that all menu items are properly and consistently prepared. Depending on the size of the operation, this could range from a coffee shop menu to a white tablecloth restaurant to room service to banquets.

Head Chef or *Chef de Cuisine*

This is the proper title for a chef who has professional cooks working for him or her. The head chef is the authority in the kitchen. In operations that do not have a certified executive chef, the head chef is ultimately responsible for all aspects of the kitchen.

Sous-Chef

The sous-chef is second in command, reports to the chef, and is in charge of the kitchen in the absence of the chef.

These three positions, executive chef, head chef, and sous-chef, constitute the administrative positions in the kitchen. As we shall see, however, the size of the restaurant or hotel will determine exactly the responsibilities of these chefs.

The Hot Line: Traditional and Contemporary Positions

The next level of work in the kitchen is that done by the various line cooks, or *chefs de partie*, who work on the hot line. The term *hot line* reflects the fact that, in most kitchens, the stoves where the hot food—soups, appetizers, entrées, vegetables, and other side dishes—is prepared for service are arranged in a line, with the various cooks working side by side. There is also a "cold line" in most kitchens.

The time spent learning your craft on the line is an invaluable part of both your overall education and the path to advancement.

Sauté Cook or *Saucier*

This position is responsible for all the sautéed items and their appropriate sauces. It is often considered the most glamorous of the spots on the line. In small operations, the work of the head chef includes that of sauté cook.

This position requires expertise not only in sautéing a variety of meats, fish, poultry, and game to their appropriate doneness, it also demands split-second timing, excellent memory skills, and the ability to keep a variety of dishes in production at one time.

The work of a modern-day sauté cook is increasingly challenging as people in the United States and Canada become more sophisticated in their tastes. The sauces of today are more often prepared *a la minute*. This means that they are prepared at the time they are ordered, rather than made in large batches and kept warm in a steam table. In addition to requiring excellent organization skills and the ability to handle more than one task at a time, the sauté cook also must have a good deal of stamina. This position requires you to stand on your feet in front of a hot stove for extended periods of time.

Grill Cook or *Grillardin*

This position is responsible for the preparation of all grilled or broiled menu items. The butcher may prepare the meats, fish, or poultry if the kitchen is large enough to have a separate position for this task. Or the meats may be cut, trimmed, tied, boned, stuffed, and marinated as necessary by the grill cook.

There are also a number of sauces that are prepared for service with grilled items; these may be prepared by the grill cook or by another station, such as the sauté cook.

Many of the same attributes necessary for work as a sauté cook are also required for the grill cook: the ability to determine proper doneness for a variety of foods, keeping a number of different orders in progress throughout service periods, and physical stamina.

If it is true that changes in American eating styles have changed the nature of the work done by the sauté cook, it is doubly true of the grill cook. In fact, many restaurants like to keep their broiler or grill station on public display. Today's grill cook is called upon to prepare everything from a traditional grilled steak to a platter of grilled vegetables.

Fish Cook or *Poissonier*

In larger kitchens, there may be a person whose sole responsibility is the preparation of fish dishes and their appropriate sauces. Frequently this position falls within the domain of the sauté cook and, in some cases, the grill cook.

Fish is not as plentiful as it once was, since the demand for fish has become so great. New findings about the nutritional benefits of fish are giving it an even greater popularity boost. The skilled fish cook must understand that he or she is dealing with an expensive and valuable commodity.

Again, the butcher may do cutting, trimming, boning, and other advance preparation of the fish. However, in many cases, this work will fall to the fish cook. It is important for the fish cook to understand the anatomy of a variety of fish and shellfish.

Pasta Cook

The pasta cook is responsible for the preparation of all pastas and noodles and their appropriate sauces. Like the fish station, this is a station that is becoming increasingly popular.

People in the United States and Canada have discovered that there is more to pasta than spaghetti and meatballs, and, consequently, this position can be extremely demanding. Delicate sauces and fresh pastas are the norm rather than the exception in high-quality restaurants and hotels.

Pastas are served as appetizers, entrées, and side dishes, so the pasta cook needs to be able to keep a number of different orders in mind at once to be sure that pastas are cooked properly and delivered to the wait staff promptly.

Vegetable Cook or *Légumier* or *Entremetier*

This position is responsible for overseeing the cleaning, trimming, cutting, and other advance preparation of all vegetables for service. Very often this position also is responsible for hot appetizers and soufflés. (There is a position in the cold kitchen or pantry that is responsible for the preparation of vegetables to be served as salads. This will be covered in Chapter 4, with the work of the pantry and *garde-manger*.)

Soup Cook or *Potager*

This position is responsible for the preparation of all ingredients for soups, stews, and braised items.

Butcher or *Boucher*

The butcher is responsible for trimming, portioning, and tying all meats and poultry, and filleting and boning fish. If there is no person whose designated position is the butcher, these duties are usually assumed by the appropriate station. For example, the fish cook will fillet and bone fish, and the sauté cook will trim and portion meats.

Fry Cook or *Friturier*

This station is responsible for the preparation of all fried items, including fritters, potatoes, and other fried dishes.

Apprentice

The position in the kitchen of apprentice, or prep person, is where most people begin their careers. The work is not highly skilled, but it is very important. This person generally cleans, trims, and prepares the vegetables for stocks, soups, and salads. This person also may be responsible for actually preparing the salads, salad dressings, and other simple menu items.

The Front of the House

Great service requires great service personnel. In an industry devoted to the culinary arts, the professional staff who directly interacts with guests is critical to the business's success. A great kitchen staff deserves a great dining room staff. For most restaurants, this means having a great dining room manager and a service staff that is constantly learning about the food being served.

You may find that your interest in the culinary arts finds its best expression in the front of the house, where you can have more direct contact with the guests. The dining room manager or banquet manager with a culinary background brings a special knowledge to her or his work. These managers are often better able to coordinate work with the kitchen to the benefit of all concerned.

Restaurants that pride themselves on their wine lists usually employ a sommelier. This expertise, married with a well-rounded knowledge of food and the culinary arts, ensures that the guests who visit the restaurant have a great array of selections. But, more importantly, it means that the sommelier is able to give each member of his or her service staff the training and information necessary to give the guest service worthy of both the wine and the food.

Summary

The restaurant kitchen, although it has changed to adapt to modern working practices, still relies on a hierarchy of responsibility. This structure not only provides a way to organize work in a kitchen, it also acts as a basic road map for developing your own career.

Every professional working in a restaurant kitchen or dining room can look to Escoffier's classic brigade system to get a better understanding of how to advance from one level to the next. The brigade, with its succinct definitions of authority and responsibility, can act as a direct line, taking you from apprentice to executive chef at a white tablecloth restaurant, or it can show the way to another area of expertise and specialization.

3

TRADITIONAL POSITIONS IN RESTAURANTS AND HOTELS

THERE IS A wide range of different restaurants in the United States and Canada today, running the gamut from expensive to family style. The work demanded by each type of restaurant will vary, depending in part upon the demands of the clientele and the menu.

As we look through the following "typical day," you will note that the references are geared to the daily operations of a white tablecloth restaurant. In these restaurants, the menu is generally a la carte, meaning that the guest can select from a variety of offerings within certain categories. The success or failure of such restaurants rests in the teamwork that exists (or doesn't exist) between the dining room and kitchen staffs.

Behind the Scenes

White tablecloth restaurants generally are considered to be the upper end of the restaurant ranking system. They are more refined, elegant, and polished than are other restaurants. They also offer service of a better quality and provide excellent (and often unusual) foods, wines, and other amenities. They tend to be more expensive for the guest and higher-paying for the staff.

The chefs and other members of the staff in these restaurants are usually highly skilled and have had a significant amount of experience working in hotel and restaurant operations where the food is of the best possible quality.

As mentioned above, menus for these restaurants are usually a la carte. The guest chooses an appetizer, soup, salad, main course, and dessert from a number of different options. When the waitperson brings the check, or "dupe," into the kitchen, the line cooks work on the order in a logical sequence, keeping in mind the information provided by the wait staff.

Here is a typical order, from the client to the kitchen and finally to the table.

"May I Take Your Order?"

A man and woman order French onion soup and paté to start their meal. Then they both will have salads. As an entrée, the woman will have the special pasta and the man will have a steak cooked rare. The waitperson writes this down on a pad or will key the order into a computer. This way the kitchen will have a record of what this table ordered, and the waitperson can make sure that the check is prepared properly at the end of the meal.

Depending on the size and type of restaurant, waitpersons or servers have a variety of job duties. In addition to taking orders, they describe special menu items and are sometimes asked to explain how an item is prepared or to suggest a wine pairing with a meal. In addition to garnishing and serving plates of food from the kitchen, sometimes waiters or waitresses carve meats or prepare special items at customers' tables.

Waitpersons must be alert and observant to anticipate customers' needs and desires and provide them with fast, efficient service. They refill water glasses or other beverage items when needed. They also watch to determine when each course has been completed. Waiters and waitresses describe and take orders for dessert or bring a tray containing a serving of each dessert to customers' tables. When the meal is complete, waiters or waitresses remove the dishes and glasses from the table and take them to the kitchen, compute the cost of the meal and prepare the check, and accept payments or refer customers to the cashier.

Timing

Cooking at home and cooking in a restaurant are two entirely different activities. Most of the day's work in a professional kitchen revolves around getting ready to serve meals during a breakfast, lunch, or dinner time period. This is known as being prepared, or *mise en place*. Having enough of every food item on hand, ready to go into the pan, and enough of the sauces, side dishes, soups, desserts, and breads that will be required constitutes a good *mise en place*.

Like the kitchen staff, the dining room staff will also spend some time getting ready to serve the guests. Side stands are stocked with condiments, napkins, extra flatware and glasses, and any other items the wait staff will require. This advance preparation is critical if the evening's service is to go smoothly.

Chefs will refer to a dish as being "fired," which is just kitchen terminology for making it. When the waitperson is certain that the table is nearly ready for a course, he or she will instruct the kitchen to "fire table 32."

In our scenario, the kitchen staff should know that the paté will take no cooking time at all, as it has been fully prepared in advance and needs only to be "plated" and garnished. The soup, however, will take some additional time, since it still needs a crouton and cheese, which is browned under a salamander or broiler. The person responsible for the cold food may decide to "plate up" the paté to have it completed and ready, and simply hold it in a cold place until the soup is ready. The soup must be started immediately.

Once the appetizers have been served, the waitperson should let the kitchen staff know when he or she is ready to pick up the salads. At the time that the salads are taken from the kitchen, the person responsible for the pasta may start that dish. The steak, which is to be cooked rare, should not be started until later, so that it will finish cooking just as it is to be served. This will allow sufficient time for the sauce to be prepared in the sauté pan.

Then the person in charge of preparing vegetables and other side dishes should be sure that there is an order of the vegetables fired for the steak, and that it will be ready at the same time that the steak is finished and plated with the sauce.

There must be constant communication between the wait staff and the kitchen staff because the scenario just described is rarely followed. One guest may decide to have two appetizers followed by a salad, while someone else at the table wants only an entrée. Or, guests at another table may want to have their meal quickly so they can go to a show or a movie, while yet another table prefers to take a more leisurely approach to the meal. Being sure that the food comes out in the proper sequence and at the correct temperature is definitely a challenge.

Once the fundamentals have been conquered, it is important to begin refining those skills. Learning to organize time, putting tasks to be accomplished in their best priority, keeping track of several tasks at one time—all of these skills can be learned only through repeated practice.

Kitchens

Keep in mind that learning the operation of one single type of kitchen does not necessarily mark an end to one's training. Each kitchen can have a different organization, different demands, different menus, and different styles of operation. In the following pages, we'll explore a few different kinds of kitchen environments in which you may find work.

Banquet Kitchens

A banquet kitchen has pressures that are far different from those found in an a la carte kitchen. In a banquet kitchen, it is necessary to feed large numbers of people at the same time and do it as quickly as possible. Foods must be prepared in large batches, as close to service time as possible. Consequently, this labor-intensive environment requires scrupulous attention to detail, unwavering control over cooking/plating activities, coordination of kitchen and dining room staffs, and a chef who is cool and poised and confident amid the multiple tasks and demands he or she faces.

A la Carte Kitchens

In an a la carte kitchen, it is a different situation completely. Adequate *mise en place* (basic stocks, sauces, soups, and other foods, ready to cook) must be kept on hand, but the actual preparation of a meal is begun only when an order comes from the dining room into the kitchen, so that all food is, as much as is feasible, cooked to order.

Commissary Kitchens

Commissary kitchens need to produce large quantities of foods and then package them appropriately so that they can withstand transportation and at least some storage time. They then can be transported to the correct site, where they will be finished close to service time.

As you can see, only your stamina and your personal interest limit the range of experiences that you could have in the culinary field. You may find that your personality and lifestyle are most complemented by work in an institutional feeding operation, such as a college food service, where the hours are predictable and holidays and weekends could be free for you to spend with your family. Or you may crave the excitement and glamour of a white tablecloth restaurant enough to sacrifice a normal working schedule and much of the free time that it often seems like everyone in the world is able to enjoy—except the chef.

As you continue through your career, you often will feel a certain amount of conflict: Should I take a job in a kitchen where I can earn a lot of money, or should I work in an operation where the pay may not be as impressive, but where I believe I can learn the most? Choosing a new job, deciding when and for what reasons you will move from one job to the next: these are all quite personal decisions. But it is difficult to go wrong if you have developed your own career path. Chiseling that path, the one that is custom-designed for you alone, is your responsibility. No one can do that for you. Learning what some of your options are is the purpose of this book.

Restaurants

Guests choose to come to a restaurant for a variety of reasons, including the style of service, the menu, and the price range. Speaking very generally, most restaurants fall into one of four categories: white tablecloth, family style, fast food, and diners.

White Tablecloth Restaurants

When guests want a dining experience, they turn to white tablecloth restaurants. They are used to calling ahead to make reservations. They expect the menu to feature dishes that require more sophistication to produce in the kitchen. These restaurants may be referred to as "destination" restaurants or special-occasion restaurants. Menus are generally more elaborate and adventurous. Patrons look for new and exciting options featuring dishes and ingredients from around the globe. Often, the chef is a personality in her or his own right. White tablecloth restaurants rely upon the successful teamwork of the highly skilled and motivated staff in the kitchen and the dining room.

White tablecloth restaurants have a heavy emphasis on foods prepared to order (known as *a la minute*), on sauces, and on more elaborate preparations and presentations. They are the showcase restaurants for hotels.

Many students graduating from culinary programs find their first jobs working in white tablecloth restaurants. A lifelong goal for some of them is to own their own restaurant.

Family-Style Restaurants

These restaurants usually have menus that appeal to families because they offer familiar food, salad bars, and low prices. The foods here are very often prepared fully or partially in a commissary, or central kitchen. The finishing steps done in the restaurant may simply include reheating the food in a microwave or finishing it by deep-frying.

Obviously these kitchens do not demand the same level of skill as a white tablecloth restaurant. However, the chef who works for the commissary kitchen has the responsibility to train all staff to prepare items to the correct standard, as well as to develop new items to keep the restaurant competitive.

Service is less demanding in these restaurants, and in many cases, the use of salad bars, soup and salad bars, and even dessert bars, further reduces the difficulty of service.

Fast-Food Restaurants

Today, fast-food restaurants are found nearly everywhere. They are in large cities, small towns, even in hospitals and schools. They may be drive-through or walk-up. Fast food doesn't necessarily have to mean burgers and fries. Different ethnic cuisines are finding their way into the mainstream. Tacos, "wraps," salads, even sushi are easier and easier to find, ready to go in minutes. The supermarket is another place you can find "fast food," with a combination of prepared foods ready to eat in the store, and fully or partially prepared foods ready to take home.

The idea is to provide food quickly and inexpensively. The foods are almost invariably prepared in a commissary or central kitchen and then simply completed at the "store," as the individual units of fast-food chains are known. This may mean that the food is reheated, portioned, or simply served as is.

There is no service in the same way that there is in a white tablecloth, or even a family-style, restaurant. Instead, there are counter workers who fill orders placed by the customer. There are no tablecloths, or even placements. The customer picks up whatever utensils might be needed—a paper napkin, plastic forks or spoons—and very often he or she also must add whatever garnish is preferred—ketchup, mustard, pickles, onions, tomatoes, hot sauce, and so forth.

Diners/Coffee Shops

These restaurants are generally looking to the breakfast and lunch crowd to make their business profitable. The idea, again, is to keep overhead low and turn tables or counter space over quickly (that is, to get people in and out of the diner as quickly as possible so that the seat that was occupied can be used by another customer).

The typical menu items associated with diners and coffee shops include sandwiches (hamburgers, grilled cheese, hot turkey, and hot meatloaf); salads and salad plates (chef salad, tuna salad, and shrimp salad); soups; and hot "blue plate specials," which are generally simple preparations such as stews, meatloaf with gravy and potatoes, turkey, or pot roast.

The foods are simply prepared without elaborate, complicated, or time-consuming sauces and accompanying side dishes. The cuts of meat generally are not as expensive, nonetheless, the proper application of technique is important. There is relatively little room to hide when preparing "plain" food for "plain folks," who know what fried chicken should taste like and can usually recognize instant mashed potatoes at ten paces.

Summary

This chapter has taken a look at the kind of work that is done in the kitchen by the person who prepares the hot food, whether it is soup, sautéed fish, grilled steak, pasta, or vegetables. There are other positions in the kitchen as well, such as bakers and the people who prepare the cold food. We will look at their work in the following chapters.

In addition to considering the kinds of jobs that are available in a typical restaurant kitchen, we also have taken a brief look at what types of restaurants there are. As you have seen, the style of service and the type of food prepared will have a direct influence on the kinds of opportunities available.

4

COLD FOODS, GARDE-MANGER, AND BANQUET WORK

IN THE SAME way that there are positions and a hierarchy of power on the hot line, so, too, are there in the cold kitchen. And the areas of responsibility in the cold kitchen are more varied than one might imagine. They include breakfast cookery (eggs, home fries, toasts, cereals, and muffins), cold salads, cold hors d'oeuvres, smoked items, marinated foods, patés, and terrines. All of these items are of great importance in most professional kitchens.

Breakfast cookery in particular has come into increasing vogue. Now, rather than being a position that is considered not quite as exalted as others in a restaurant or hotel, it has become one of the more intriguing and challenging options open to a cook or chef.

Breakfast Cook

As busy people in the United States and Canada turn more and more to restaurants for their morning meal, and as "power breakfasts" become a way of life for businesspeople everywhere, the breakfast a hotel or restaurant offers becomes of increasing importance. Not so long ago, "eggs any style, choice of bacon or sausage, home fries, juice, and coffee" were all anyone really needed to know about breakfast. This is no longer true, and with the steady popularity of brunch, the situation shows no signs of changing.

One of the reasons that breakfast has become so important is that many people who have a full round of business meetings are choosing to start their days early. They meet with their personal trainer or go for a run before seven o'clock, and then start the first meeting of the day at breakfast. The ability to accommodate these "power breakfasters" can make or break a reputation.

The talented breakfast chef of today must possess the same skills as a sauté cook. The ability to prepare several items at once, with split-second timing, is of paramount importance. Breakfast is generally not as leisurely a meal as dinner or even lunch.

The range of foods that must be prepared for breakfast also calls a number of skills into play. There are hot cereals, eggs in a variety of styles, vegetables, fruit compotes and fruit plates, blintzes, pancakes, crepes, waffles, muffins, and other breads as well. These are items that, for the most part, need to be prepared as close as possible to service time. And as consumers become ever more flexible in their understanding of what constitutes breakfast food, the chance for creativity is constantly expanding.

Pantry Cook

Until quite recently, this was one of the few stations, along with the bakeshop, that was traditionally staffed by women. Today, it can be an extremely challenging position that calls for talented and creative individuals with no reference at all to sex or race.

The responsibilities of the pantry cook will change depending upon the type of operation. In general, however, this station is responsible for preparing a wide range of salads, salad dressings, cold hors d'oeuvres and appetizers, and cold desserts.

If there is no formal banquet kitchen, the pantry cook also may assist the chef in determining what types of foods would be appropriate for a reception or buffet. The challenge to produce attractive, appealing foods while keeping food costs low is one that the truly skilled pantry cook will meet again and again. For some people, it is like solving an infinitely challenging and constantly changing puzzle.

Butcher or Boucher

The butcher is responsible for a wide variety of food preparations, and though it is less common to find this as a separate station in all but the largest operations, a well-trained butcher can find a position virtually anywhere in the country. Specialty butchering is a skill that is harder and harder to find, while at the same time demand is growing for meats that are trimmed and cut in such a way as to keep them in line with current standards.

The butcher is responsible for portioning, trimming, tying, trussing, butterflying, and stuffing, as required by the type of meat. Each steak, cutlet, chop, or piece of chicken will be custom-cut to suit the needs of the operation or the particular recipe.

In addition to preparing beef, pork, veal, lamb, and poultry, the butcher also may be responsible for a wide range of variety meats, including brains, oxtails, marrow bones, and sweetbreads (the thymus gland of a calf). Game, an increasingly popular item on many menus, will require butchering, too. It also may be necessary to "hang" game (hold it in a controlled environment until it ripens), if the style of cookery in a particular establishment calls for that.

The responsibility for carefully butchering meat extends beyond being sure that the meat is trimmed of fat, silverskin, and gristle and cut into the correct portion size. It is here that a great deal of money can be made or lost. The skilled butcher cuts meats in such a way as to lose as little usable meat as possible.

For example, if the butcher cuts a leg of veal carefully, he or she will be able to produce the maximum number of cutlets. The trim meat can then be used for stew meat, or it may be ground for the garde-manger chef to use in stuffings (known as forcemeat) or other dishes. The bones will be cut down and used, along with any trim that cannot be used for stews or forcemeat, to prepare stocks and sauces.

The butcher also may be responsible for preparing fish to be cooked. This involves scaling, gutting, filleting (removing skin and bones), and portioning. The fish also will be stuffed, if necessary, cut into steaks, and so forth. Shellfish may require portioning, or it may need to be shucked to serve on the half shell.

Obviously, the amount and type of work done by a skilled butcher is varied. But in many operations, there is no butcher. This means that some other position, either the chef or one of the line cooks, will assume this work. Or, it may mean that the restaurant will opt to buy its meats and fish already trimmed and cut into portion sizes. The additional cost may be warranted if there is no one with enough skill to perform this work, but the added cost to the meats and fish purchased in this way can be very great indeed.

Garde-Manger Chef

The chef in charge of the cold station must be able to prepare a wide range of foods, and often this station also will be responsible for the butchering of meats and fish, unless there is a separate butcher station. (Usually it is only very large operations that will have a separate butcher station, as explained earlier.)

The garde-manger chef has a number of responsibilities. He or she must understand which foods are best when prepared in a cold fashion, how and when to marinate foods, how smokers work, what the effect of brining and smoking would be on the food, and how to best arrange and display the items.

Banquet Chef

The banquet chef for a hotel is in charge of a very important area of the hotel's business. Many operations count on conventions, meetings, and special events such as weddings, bar mitzvahs, and receptions to generate a large part of their revenue. The banquet chef is crucial to the success or failure of this part of the operation.

The banquet chef is responsible for developing a number of different menus that can then be adjusted to meet the special needs or requirements of the guests. The menu must be carefully priced so that the customer perceives the value that he or she is getting, and also so that the greatest possible amount of profit is generated from the event. It is usually easier to meet a desirable profit margin when you know in advance how many people will be dining, at exactly what time, and on exactly which evening. An a la carte restaurant chef does not have this luxury.

The ability to carefully organize an incredible number of details is paramount. This might include making sure that there are enough tables for a buffet or enough champagne tulips to serve during the intermezzo; hiring or preparing an ice carving; and coordinating with the bakeshop to make sure that the roses on the wedding cake are the same color as the linens, which should be the same color as the bridesmaids' gowns.

In a very large hotel, it is entirely possible that there may be several different events taking place on the same day. Dovetailing all the advance preparation and the actual cooking and service of the food is a job that requires enormous reserves of concentration, endurance, and skill.

On-Premise Catering

When there are large parties or banquets to be produced by a kitchen, the banquet chef must be able to coordinate many activities. He or she will determine what sort of hors d'oeuvres would be appropriate for a reception. He or she also must be able to arrange various styles of buffets, knowing that what might be correct for a cocktail reception following an opening at the museum will not work for a wedding reception. The chef must be able to present the food in a graceful and appropriate fashion as well as decide how best to serve the food, whether that would be by passing the items "butler" style or by arranging them in a buffet display.

The menu must be determined in advance and be suitable to the occasion. If hors d'oeuvres are included, they should harmonize with the foods being served later. And they must be attractive enough to entice guests to try them, without being so large or so heavy that the meal that follows cannot be enjoyed.

To get a better idea of what would occur during an in-house catered affair, let's look at a typical party, in this case, a wedding reception.

Banquet Chef as Marketing Specialist and Salesperson

The couple, or more likely the bride and her mother, arrive to discuss booking your dining room for the wedding reception. They may or may not have set a firm date. You will need to go over the possible dates for the event, what hours they have in mind, and a host of other questions.

Depending upon your operation, you may be able to offer a full or limited bar, a disc jockey or house band, a flower service, a house photographer, or a host of other special items. Ideally, you will able to sell the wedding as a package. Once you have established the date and time, you need to begin to consider the menu.

Very often people will come to you expecting that you will guide them. Many banquet chefs will have prepared a number of different menus and figured out the selling price for the banquet ahead of time. If this is the case, you can go over these options with the client.

One area that will make a big difference in the final calculation of price is the number of guests. Very often this is only an estimate in the early stages, and it will have to be finalized closer to the date of the affair. Clients frequently will have one or more special requests that you will need to factor into the price of the wedding reception. Or they may ask for an entire menu that is not currently part of your repertoire. You will need to do the necessary research to find out what the food will cost and how much you will have to charge to make a profit on the affair. You also must factor into the cost of the reception the following:

- Additional kitchen or wait staff prior to and on the day of the event
- Any cost to you for the rental of equipment, china, linen, and glassware
- Flowers, if you are providing them
- Music, if you are providing it

- The wedding cake
- Any other options that you may decide to offer as a part of your package

Banquet Chef as Personnel Director and Purchasing Steward

As the day of the event draws closer, you will need to schedule staff—perhaps even additional staff—according to the number of guests to be served at the reception and the style of service desired.

If there are a number of hors d'oeuvres, they may need to be made in advance and properly stored. You might have to schedule additional time or staff to accomplish these goals. It is important to have a prioritized list of responsibilities prepared and a clear idea of where the progress of the event must be on any given day.

Since you will not actually purchase the foods, wines, beer, and other items until you have a more certain count of the guests, you may choose not to order much of the product required until you are close to the big day. But you should have, at least in a general sense, an idea of how much you will need to buy to feed the people attending the event. And you should have done some additional research to determine which of your purveyors is most likely to provide the best quality at the best price.

The ideal is to purchase enough food to feed everyone generously, but not so much that there is a large amount of waste. No one can afford waste, since it cuts into your own profit margin. The trick of getting the food in sync with the number of guests is a skill that comes only with time, and even then, the risk of over- or underpurchasing is constant.

Banquet Chef as Chef and Manager

On the day of the event, you are the master of ceremonies in far more than name. If there is a burned-out light or a missing coatrack, chances are good that your name is the one that will be called. It is essential that the preliminary work be completed so that you will have time to work through the disasters that may come up. Any banquet chef could regale you for hours with stories of near misses, and worse. They may be funny after time has passed, but when a hysterical bride is staring you in the eye, the humor in the situation seems nonexistent.

Because most celebrations are firmly rooted in food, it will be the duty of the kitchen, and hence the banquet chef, to set the pace of the event. The style and type of hors d'oeuvre service can be altered even during the course of the reception to allow more time or to speed the process along. For example, if the bridal party is taking longer at the church than anticipated, you will need to adjust the service of hors d'oeuvres so that they will not be completely gone by the time the wedding party does arrive. However, you will have to serve enough so that the guests are not completely starved by that time.

Buffet-style service should be arranged carefully so that the guests can walk easily around the buffet and back to their tables. There must be easy access to all foods, without having to reach over other dishes; this and a number of other considerations need to be kept in mind.

If the meal were to be served "sit down," you would, of course, have arranged for a suitable number of wait staff so that service is not slowed down. You would want to be sure that everyone gets their food as quickly as possible to avoid the problem of several tables being done eating while other tables have not yet received their food.

One of the final moments of concern for the banquet chef is the service of the wedding cake. It is important that there be enough time for a proper ceremony, pictures, and all the rest. But at the same time, it is important that the kitchen or wait staff be able to dispense the cake to the guests as quickly as possible.

Off-Premise Catering

The situation described above, though a nerve-racking kind of event for even the most unflappable of persons, is usually much easier to plan and go through if you are working in your own facility. You know how many ovens and stoves you have, and you probably have an established list of wait staff and additional kitchen staff. Now, let's look at the other type of catering: catering done at a place that is far removed from your kitchen.

In addition to the steps for the reception outlined above, you also will need to visit the site to determine what kind of equipment you will have available, and whether you can devise a menu that will allow you to pull the event off without transporting portable refrigerators and stoves to the site.

You undoubtedly will need to rent chairs, tables, linen, china, and all the other necessary accoutrements for the event. If it is to be held outside, you will have to decide if there should be tents. You also will have to look the site over carefully to determine if there will be sufficient parking for your staff, and very likely the guests as well. You may need to bring in portable toilets. The amount of detail work required to come up with a list of rental items and the menu is staggering, unless you are extremely organized.

You also need to be able to visualize the entire affair from beginning to end, mentally walking through all the phases of the reception. By doing that, you may find that you forgot to order trays or ice tubs for the drinks, beverage napkins, or enough forks to get through a salad course, the entrée, and the dessert. If you are planning to give champagne to four hundred people and don't have champagne glasses, the chances of finding someone able to bail you out at the last moment are slim. But if you rehearse how the party will run, you will raise a champagne glass to give a toast, compare that action against one of your many lists, and realize the problem in time to avert disaster.

Kosher Catering

One area of specialization for caterers is kosher catering. In addition to all of the qualities required of any caterer or banquet chef, the kosher caterer also must be able to prepare foods that meet the dietary laws. The requirements are clearly spelled out, but they may be unfamiliar to many caterers. The chances of committing a minor or major faux pas are great. Even greater concern with detail and closer attention to menu planning may be required to ensure that your guests are pleased with their event.

Summary

Breakfast cooks, salad cooks, pantry cooks, banquet chefs, and caterers—we have seen in this chapter just how important they are to the success of many operations. People who chose to work in this area of the culinary arts find great reward in their ability to bring off an event perfectly, the same way that actors get a natural high from a good performance.

If you enjoy being on display, then this area could be the perfect one for you. But as you can see, you owe it to yourself to test the waters, and test yourself. The physical and emotional demands of working in banquets, making canapés for three thousand people or preparing one hundred perfect sunny-side-up eggs, are great. But then, so are the rewards and the satisfactions.

5

BAKING AND PASTRY

BAKERS, BAKERS' ASSISTANTS, and pastry chefs very often are considered specialists. There has been a tendency in the past to divide the kitchen so completely that it is not unusual to have pastry chefs profess total ignorance of what goes on in other parts of the kitchen.

Some young chefs turn to baking and pastry after spending some time or getting training in the hot kitchen. They can tell you they find that the underlying principles are the same. Still, time spent in the hot kitchen is not essential. If you know that the bakeshop is where your talents and your interests are, you should tailor your education and training so that you can get the most benefit out of your time spent in school or as an apprentice.

It is undeniably true that a good chef must be well versed in all areas of the kitchen, including the bakeshop. His or her ability to work with a variety of pastry doughs, mousses, and other mixtures more commonly associated with the bakeshop is a good indicator of how serious his or her commitment to excellence is.

It is equally true that some people will find that they are more drawn to work in the bakeshop than they are to work in the kitchen. There are a number of differences between life as a pastry chef and life as an executive or head chef. However, there is no difference in the respect to which those who have reached the upper levels of either branch of the culinary arts are entitled.

A Renaissance in Bread Baking

A quick look through the yellow pages of the phone book, the offerings in your local bookstore, or the word-of-mouth information you may come across will prove that not only are bakeshops still alive, they are gaining in recognition and prestige. Small and not-so-small bakeries are producing some exceptional artisanal breads, using a combination of traditional and modern techniques. The goal to produce handcrafted, hearth-baked breads has been embraced by a variety of individuals. Daniel Leader of Boiceville, New York's Bread Alone Bakery, Amy's Breads, Tom Cat Bakery, and other local and national producers have shown that bread is worth extra effort, time, and money.

Bakeshops are noted primarily for their production of muffins, quick breads, yeast breads, rolls, and simple desserts. Although this generally is not considered glamorous work, it is work that demands skill, creativity, and the ability to produce large amounts of products quickly and efficiently.

Quick breads, muffins, and other simple batters are relatively easy to prepare, but a bakeshop can make or break its reputation on its quality. Since bakeshops are traditionally open early in the morning, people will get in the habit of stopping by for a bran muffin and coffee on the way to work—that is, if your bran muffins are the best in town. And if they really like your goods, customers will most likely stop by on the way home, too, for a loaf of bread for dinner or a pie for dessert.

Bakers must be able to scale (or measure) ingredients accurately, mix them properly, and bake them correctly. This is not just a simple matter of following a formula. On any given day, the air may be more humid or the flour may be a little harder or dryer than the last batch was. Only bakers who are skilled enough to see or feel the difference in dough and make the correct adjustments can ensure consistency.

Many large-scale bakeshops use machines to mix and shape doughs. This makes for greater uniformity of product.

The Bakeshop "Brigade"

The chain of command in a bakeshop is actually not all that different from what it is in a kitchen. There is a head baker and assistant baker and then as many additional workers as necessary to meet the daily production quota.

The hours for a baker are rigorous, just as they are for most other people working in the culinary arts. Bakers, however, usually start their work before the sun comes up and finish about the time that chefs who work the dinner shift are coming in to work.

There are bakeshops that do the work from start to finish, and there are those that purchase products that are partially prepared. One bakeshop will have its own "secret" formulas for breads, muffins, and cupcakes. Others will purchase frozen doughs and finish baking them. In either case, the level of expertise required from the workers will determine how well they are paid.

Many hotels and supermarkets, and even some fast-food chains that offer fresh-baked biscuits, will have to do at least some of the baking directly on the premises. Although this is often nothing more complicated than adding the required amount of liquid to a prepared mix, others will make more complicated items such as Danishes or doughnuts that require filling, frosting, and glazing.

Fine Pastries and Plated Desserts

Pastry shops are responsible for preparing the more elaborate baked items. These include small French pastries, elaborate cakes, wedding cakes, candies, and other specialty items.

The work that is done in pastry shops is even more exacting than that done in a bakeshop. The creations that are produced require a certain sense of form, line, and balance. These are the creations that cause people to stop in their tracks.

Working with chocolate and sugar are among the special skills that pastry chefs must have. These talents take a great deal of time, training, patience, and practice.

It is not unusual for a trained chef to decide to move into this demanding and specialized field. Quite often, he or she will elect to continue his or her training, either by attending a school that is dedicated to teaching this craft or by working closely with a respected pastry chef.

Just as there are certified executive chefs and certified master chefs, there are also certified master pastry chefs. This honor is bestowed on those people who have completed the required and rigorous course of studies and examinations, coupled with the appropriate experience.

Where Can I Work?

There are many places to either hone or put your skills to work in this area of the culinary arts. Depending on your preferences, you can work for large commercial operations, smaller in-house shops, or specialty shops.

Commercial Bakeries

Large bakeries that produce breads, cookies, and other baked goods employ large numbers of bakers. However, not all of these bakers need to be especially skilled. The large batches that are produced are made according to carefully developed formulas. The mixing, kneading, shaping, rising, and baking of bread, for instance, is usually carefully controlled and monitored by sophisticated equipment. Today, it often is computerized to ensure that the quality and consistency of the product is exactly maintained.

Nonetheless, there is no substitute for humans in some areas, particularly when it comes to developing new products. The formulas that will be used to create the large quantities often start off as family recipes that were found on special trips to Europe to search out new ideas. Or they may very well be completely new developments.

Then, the real work begins. The formula must be continually revised until the product reaches its final stages. At that point, it is ready to go out for test marketing and, finally, full-scale production.

In-House Bakeshops and Pastry Shops

It is often a mark of superior quality if a restaurant can claim, truthfully, that its breads, pastries, and desserts are all prepared from scratch on the premises. Reputations can be made or lost on the basis of how good a piece of cake or other dessert is.

It certainly is possible to buy almost anything prepared. Cheesecakes, tortes, pies, and ice creams are all available from purveyors.

Today, it is even possible to purchase prepared soufflés; all you have to do is bake them in the oven. But, if a restaurant or hotel can afford to offer its guests truly fresh muffins, bagels, breads, and other bakery items, the difference is something that even less discriminating customers can appreciate.

Many restaurants today set aside at least part of their kitchen space for bakery work. It often is possible to work around the schedule of the rest of the kitchen; the baker can work on days that the restaurant is closed, in the period between lunch and dinner, or after the dinner hour is over.

Specialty Work and Entrepreneurs

There are stores in most small and large cities that offer specialty items, such as chocolates, eclairs, Napoleons, and special cakes, to name just a few. Some shops sell their wares exclusively to restaurants, hotels, and other fine dining establishments. Others are open to the public.

The production of wedding cakes is one area that specialty bakeshops often excel at. This is a very particular type of work, calling for a number of skills and talents. Not all of these talents are strictly related to the actual baking of the cake and mixing of the icing. It also is important to have an artistic sense, the flair to create beautiful things from butter cream, marzipan, chocolate, or royal icing. These ingredients are the special "paints" or "clays" that pastry chefs use to create their works of art.

Many people who do not want to work full-time in a bakeshop prepare cakes, pies, and other items in their homes. They may do this for only one or two restaurants, producing their "signature" items, or they may work with a caterer or catering house to prepare the desserts and pastries for special events.

Of course, it is important to be sure that if you choose to work from your home, you have adequate space to store both raw materials and finished goods, plenty of refrigeration, large counters or workbenches, and enough heavy-duty equipment to mix and bake the items. You also need to make sure that you have met all codes, applied for all licenses and permits, and are operating in a safe, clean fashion.

Professional Development for Bakers and Pastry Chefs

Just as there are special competitions for chefs, there are also competitions for bakers and pastry chefs, and they most often are held at the same time.

These competitions give pastry chefs the opportunity to stretch their creative talents a little more and to hone their skills. It also is a chance to see what other people in the field are doing. As there are plenty of "fads," styles that come and go, it is important to keep on top of these changes.

Nutritional cooking has had an influence on the kinds of items that are prepared by bakers, from reducing the amount of heavy cream, eggs, and butters in desserts to preparing breads that are high in fiber and low in sodium. All of these changes should be looked at as challenges.

Summary

Baking is a special craft, and pastry is an art. The people who create the breads, pies, cakes, and confections that start people drooling simply by looking at them have a unique talent.

Bakeshops are not identical; there are situations to suit nearly any personality and any level of skill. There are commercial bakeries, in-house bakeries, pastry shops, and the talented craftspeople who specialize in chocolate, pulled sugar, and other fine work. The key to success is to find a job that allows you to use your talents to the fullest.

6

CULINARY CAREERS IN NONTRADITIONAL SETTINGS

Up to this point in our discussion of culinary careers, we have focused primarily on work that could bring you into contact with a relatively large public. The work outlined in this chapter is slightly different in its approach. The chef who works in private placement or consultation may operate on a one-to-one basis, similar to a personal trainer. In fact, with the advent of the new century, there may be a growing demand for chefs who can work for a single family, tailoring the diet to suit special, individual needs.

Private Chef

The first family has a private chef, and so does the mayor of New York City. There are plenty of other individuals and families who employ private chefs, and they are not all high-ranking political officials. The reasons for hiring a private chef in the first place may vary from situation to situation. The responsibilities and salaries offered also will vary.

The chef to a family may find it necessary to tailor or modify meals to suit the needs of a special diet or prescribed nutritional program, or simply to gratify the tastes and expectations of the family or individual. In addition to cooking for the family, he or she also will prepare any dinner parties or large receptions held by the family. In some households, this may mean a small dinner party twice a year; in other households, it may mean several receptions of one hundred to two hundred people or more throughout the year.

There is seldom a perfectly reliable schedule to all of this work. It may be that you will find yourself on call. Let's imagine that the couple you work for goes out to a party and comes home very late at night. They may find it convenient to wake you so that you can prepare them omelets. Or, you may have enough food in the house to make lunch for the couple, their children, and the two guests who were there for breakfast, only to find out that several other friends dropped by in the course of the morning. You must be able to remain incredibly flexible, as well as being truly ingenious, when it comes to repeating the miracle of the loaves and fishes.

Your function may include other responsibilities. For example, the duty of doing all the shopping for the household may fall to you. And in addition to overseeing the operation of the kitchen, you also may function as the steward or majordomo. This means that you might be the one who makes out schedules and manages the operation of the entire household staff.

Or, you may be looked to as the sommelier. This means that you should be able to match wines to the foods selected for a particular menu. You also may be looked to for advice or guidance in selecting and purchasing wines for the cellar.

Menu planning may be strictly your domain, or you may work in conjunction with the family. It always will be necessary to suit the menu to the personal likes and dislikes of the family members, as well as their guests. Many people will require or prefer a special diet, vegetarian or low in sodium and cholesterol, for example. It becomes increasingly important to know how to meet the expectations of your employer without repeating a cycle of meals in an endless rotation.

Entertaining may well take up a large portion of your time. It may mean hiring additional staff and coordinating florists, musicians, and a host of other people hired for a particular occasion. The ability to stay organized in the face of overwhelming chaos may well be one of the most valuable tools you can bring to the job.

Working for a family is not for everyone. The benefits may be great. There is a chance that you will travel to beautiful, exotic places. You may find that you are actually working for the family for what amounts to no more than one-third to one-fourth of the year. But, unlike a restaurant where you can get up and go at the end of the day, you most likely will live in the house, or near enough that you can be available almost on a moment's notice. You may occasionally feel that you have become more of a caretaker than a chef, responsible for packing school lunches and picking up dry cleaning and other domestic chores that simply are not part of the job description for someone working in a restaurant or hotel.

Look carefully at what the trade-offs will be before making a decision. This type of work is incredibly fulfilling and rewarding under the right circumstances and with the right personalities involved. By all means, however, take the time to ask a lot of questions and let the family find out about you, too.

Chef on a Yacht

This sounds like one of the most alluring jobs that you could ever find. Imagine yourself drifting along on the beautiful Caribbean Sea, dropping anchor off an exotic island, and preparing exotic foods with mangoes and papayas.

Just to be fair though, consider this picture, too. You are at sea for long stretches, and keeping food fresh in a tiny galley with limited refrigeration and storage is going to be a serious concern. The people on board, whether they own the boat or simply have rented it, will consider meals as one of their favorite forms of entertainment. You can't go very far or do very much on a boat, and neither can they. The sea can get choppy, and the food is as likely to take a spill on the floor as the charts are. In this situation, you also should realize that you couldn't take a day off. While you are actually sailing around on the ocean, you will be on call—all day, every day.

Now that you have considered some of the downsides, think again about the sea breezes, the exotic ports of call, and the thrill of living on a boat. Most chefs who work on charter boats can decide which cruises they will take and how long they will be at sea. You can have at least a little control over how much of your life is spent as a galley slave. And, if you work on very large boats, you will not be alone in the galley.

So if it still sounds worth the trouble, look into it. There is almost always an opportunity, because the romance of sea life is not always enough for everyone when they face its reality. For others, though, it is enough.

Executive Dining Rooms

The opportunity to work as the chef for an executive dining room may be perfectly suited to some people. The hours are generally regular, and they seldom will extend past the lunch hour. The number of people you will be cooking for is often quite small.

Many of the same requirements demanded of a private chef also are necessary to be successful when working as the chef for an executive dining room. Here, too, you must accommodate the needs and desires of a select group of readily identifiable personalities. The style of the company may be reflected in the kinds of foods preferred in the lunchroom. A young, contemporary business may favor trendy foods. A conservative, well-established corporation may cling to the traditions of a men's club—red meat, not too many vegetables, and cold martinis. Or, the company may prefer a simple approach to its meals.

It is essential to be able to tailor the foods and menu items to the group of people you will be serving. And it is equally important to keep in mind that time is a critical commodity in almost every aspect of business. The meals must be served punctually. In cases where business is conducted during the meal, there also must be a minimum of disruption from the wait staff. More than likely it will be preferable to select foods that won't make a mess out of business papers and silk ties. Look upon it as a challenge!

Working as a chef for an executive dining room may not offer as many opportunities to impress a large audience as you might have working for a restaurant or a hotel. However, there are a great many more holidays and weekends open for you to spend with your family or friends. For some people, this type of position represents a chance to continue their educations or to branch out slowly into business for themselves.

The position of chef for an executive dining room may not always be easy to obtain; these aren't the kinds of openings that find their way into the want ads.

Chef to the Stars

If glamour by association is appealing to you, then this is an area that might be worth looking into. As actors, musicians, and other "beautiful people" are jumping on the health and fitness bandwagon, hiring personal trainers to travel with them to exotic locales and keep them from losing their strength or shape, they also are giving a nod to the other side of the coin. They are looking for people who can either travel with them or be hired on location to prepare the foods that will keep them healthy and fit.

There are chefs and caterers who provide the food for an entire film company during the production of a film, and when they cannot be found in the exact location, they may be brought in. The contracts for many performers who go out on tour may specify exactly what kinds of foods they will want available, and when. It is the responsibility of the caterer to make sure that those needs are met.

Chef as the Star

Open up any newspaper from a major metropolitan area, especially on a Wednesday. Whether it is called "Lifestyle," "Food," "Cooking," or "Home," you will most likely find plenty of space devoted to food and cooking. There are also entire magazines devoted to food, for example, *Saveur, Gourmet, Food and Wine, Bon Appetit,* and *Eating Well,* that typically showcase established or rising "star" chefs.

Turn on the television and flip to PBS, the Home and Garden channel, the Food Network, the Discovery Channel, and local access. Chances are good you won't have to wait long for a cooking show. Go straight to the Food Network if you don't want to wait. It's all food, all the time! This is a natural move for a chef who is truly passionate about food.

The idea that anyone can simply show up at a television studio with some knives and a good soufflé recipe and be a star is pretty far-fetched now. The superstar chef got that way by working hard, not just at learning about cooking, but also at promoting himself or herself. That is the reason for the television show, the benefit appearance, the cooking contest, the newspaper column, or the glossy, coffee-table cookbook.

The trend toward chef as star has not dissipated over time; in fact, it seems to grow stronger with each year. There is something about cooking that has captured our imagination as a society. Young chefs today grow up with dreams of becoming personalities and celebrities such as Emeril Lagasse, Sara Moulton, Bobby Flay, and Mario Batali. Star status doesn't come automatically, no matter how fabulous the chef's cooking might be, and it is not something that every chef aspires to. Many might tell you that the demands on their time and attention were not worth losing their connection to cooking for their guests and working with their staff. Others have found that a quick rise to celebrity is nothing more than the proverbial fifteen minutes of fame if they didn't have the solid culinary underpinnings of the "stars" with staying power.

Consulting

Consultation can run the gamut. It may mean that you will be hired by a restaurant to review a menu and assist in giving it a face-lift, or even major surgery. You may be hired by an individual to help get a new diet off and running. Or a corporate dining facility might need some help training employees to prepare new menu items.

Companies that develop or manufacture cooking equipment often look for individuals to help demonstrate their wares at shows and other events throughout the country. Your responsibility may be nothing greater than to show up on time and run through a prepared script. Or you may be looked to for guidance. You may develop recipes to demonstrate new cooking equipment to its best advantage, and perhaps even produce a small pamphlet or training video to help the company promote its product.

Once again, these positions are not likely to be found in the help-wanted section of the newspaper listed under "Cook" or "Chef." But a little research on your part, keeping informed and abreast of new models of equipment developed for both consumer and professional use, will start to give you a sense of who might be in the market for this type of consulting service. Going to trade shows will also help.

Summary

Finding a job as a chef in the private sector can take more effort than finding other types of jobs. You may have to work through an agency, or you may have to rely on word of mouth since these jobs are not usually advertised. And it does take a certain temperament to make a go of it. You may find, after a time, that you feel stifled

or even trapped working for the same two, three, or four people day in and day out.

However, you may find that this is the perfect chance to let your creativity soar. The chance to create a new menu daily with only the market as your limit, or a few pet peeves or allergies to set the boundaries, might be the kind of environment that makes you happiest.

There is no typical private placement job. You may be simply the cook, with relatively little interaction with the family that you feed. Or, you may become an invaluable part of the household, a special family member. It can be quite a challenge to have to pick up and go to a foreign country when the family decides to go on vacation, but if you find the idea appealing, look into it some more and give it a try.

7

COOKING FOR SPECIAL NEEDS

THERE IS AN increasing interest in healthy lifestyles. The ground-swell of interest in physical fitness that began in the seventies has blossomed into a way of life for an ever-growing number of people. In this chapter, we will look at some of the ways that this has changed how people spend their leisure time, and what they are hoping to be able to accomplish through a healthy diet. The opportunities for charting your own path are exciting, new, and limited only by the amount of energy and imagination you are willing to put forth.

Diets

The reasons that people adopt a particular diet are many. Their doctors may have insisted that they go on a low-cholesterol diet. They may have developed diabetes. They may have severe food allergies. Or they may simply be interested in incorporating the latest nutritional findings into their own diets to help prevent the onset of dis-

eases or delay the signs of aging. As more research is done, these findings change, and the changes can have far-reaching impact on what people should (or think they should) be eating.

The first thing to keep in mind is this: there is no replacement for a thorough and comprehensive understanding of the basics of nutrition. You will better understand every diet or eating plan if you learn about the basic concepts it relies on. For example, if you know that the Atkins diet calls for lots of protein-rich foods, you'll be better able to find appropriate foods that aren't listed in the Atkins diet itself but that actually do meet the diet's standards.

Take courses in basic nutrition and, if possible, consider getting a degree in nutrition. If you do go on for a degree, realize that there is a great deal of biology and chemistry that will be involved. Computers play an increasingly important role in nutrient and diet analysis and in unraveling the complexities of devising a menu.

There are some fundamental principles that need to be understood. These are equally important whether you are offering a service or whether you will be primarily concerned with preparing and serving the food.

The first principle is this: keep abreast of the most current recommendations from the USDA, the American Heart Association, the American Cancer Society, the American Dietetic Association, and other organizations dedicated to nutritional research and education. These are the findings that make their way into the nightly news and national magazines.

Second, learn what the dietary guidelines are for your clientele's preferred diet. Trendy diet plans come and go quickly, though most seem to fall into one of the following categories: restricted calories; low-fat and high carbohydrate; high protein and low carbohydrate. Vegetarian diets cover the gamut, ranging from veganism to pesco

(fish eating) or lacto-ovo (dairy and egg eating) vegetarians who occasionally enjoy a steak. Macrobiotic and detoxifying diets are among the options turned to by those who are faced with a medical condition such as heart disease or diabetes. Some diets may avoid certain foods altogether or call for specific combinations of food to be eaten at specific times. In some cases, you may need to introduce a wide range of unfamiliar foods. In others, you may have a relatively small universe of ingredients to work with. The more restricted a diet is, the more you need to approach cooking with a mission to prepare and present food items in ways that showcase their goodness and make them attractive. This means, of course, buying the freshest, highest quality ingredients you can find. You may need to find ways to make small portions look large for those making a switch from a meat-and-potatoes diet. Diets that severely limit food choices pose another challenge: finding ways to make or present the too-familiar food in new ways.

There is a significant change in the way chefs go about "healthy" or "diet" cooking today. Instead of focusing on what needs to be removed from the plate, they are concentrating on finding dishes that are so appealing and delicious that the client consuming the chef's tasty food isn't even aware he or she is eating "diet" food.

The types of services you might offer clients can be quite diverse. A few of these are discussed here.

Shopping and Meal Planning Service

In this case, clients should tell you clearly their preferences, needs, and any special concerns. After an initial review of the foods that they currently eat that fit in with the diet program outlined by their doctor or a trained nutritionist, you might then go into their

kitchens to get a feel for what kinds of foods they have on hand. Some people offering this kind of service may actually "clean house," removing all the "bad" foods and outfitting the kitchen with a completely new "good" pantry, refrigerator, and freezer.

After this initial work is completed, the service may develop a weekly menu, which then generates a shopping list. The food is purchased, delivered, and unpacked.

This type of service is gaining in popularity, especially in larger metropolitan areas. Family units in which both partners are involved in their careers often want the satisfaction of preparing meals, but they simply do not have the time that it takes to sit down and plan out a week's menu, and then do the necessary shopping. The number of clients that your service can handle will depend on how well you can organize your work and dovetail shopping and delivery schedules.

You need to have the necessary creativity to devise weekly menus for the same client week in and week out, month in and month out, without repeating the same dishes over and over. Nothing is less appealing than a steady diet of plain chicken breast, rice, steamed broccoli, and poached pears.

You may find that you need to learn more about special ingredients or ethnic cuisines. It may help to find out what kind of restaurants your clients enjoy, what their favorite comfort foods are, and anything else that can help you in the all-important work of coming up with those meal plans.

Menu Planning and Meal Preparation Service

Many of the same requirements noted above apply here as well, with the important addition that the food is already prepared, fully or partially, when it is delivered to the house. This means that the

client will simply reheat the entrée—usually in a microwave—toss the prepared salad greens with the prepared salad dressing, and put dinner on platters or plates.

It is important to assess how much time and preparation you will need to spend on each client. Making enough stock or soup to deliver to your clients will take about the same amount of time to prepare whether you are making a batch for ten or a batch for thirty. But when you have to debone, skin, trim, and pound chicken breasts, each one takes the same amount of time, multiplied by the number of times you have to do it.

This service also may require that you make deliveries twice or even three times throughout the week, to be sure that the food is at the peak of freshness, flavor, and quality. The added travel time is something that needs to be accounted for when you work out your own schedule.

Cooking for a Spa

Some areas of the country are growing increasingly attracted to the notion that you can find a person to make sure that you do your exercises and eat the right foods at the right time. This is a service that offers the best of all "health" worlds.

A personal exercise trainer makes sure that the appropriate type and amount of exercise is geared specifically to the abilities and needs of an individual. And since health is a question of balance, it is important that this toned and strengthened body is fed the right nutrients in the right proportions and at the right time.

A spa is often the first thing that comes to mind when the topic is nutritional cooking. It is certainly a challenge, first of all to find a job in a spa, and then to meet the carefully constructed regulations of the diet it follows.

Depending upon the philosophy of the spa, the needs and expectations of the clients, and the level of activity that the participants are expected to meet, the number of calories allotted per day can range from under one thousand to around fifteen hundred or more. The number of meals and snacks served each day will play a big role in what kinds of foods you prepare and what the portion sizes will be like.

Spas today are usually intended to do far more than act as a "fat farm" where, at one time, primarily women came to check in for a week of semistarvation, carrot sticks, and facials. The intention today at many spas is to rejuvenate, learn new exercise and relaxation techniques, and completely reorient eating habits. The lessons learned at the spa are supposed to travel with the client (women and men) into their everyday world. Food that wouldn't keep a rabbit's interest is certainly not the answer.

Many spas have become famous for the quality of their food. The chef and his or her staff are often deluged with requests for recipes, and some have written programs that can be taken with the client back to the real world. The emphasis in most successful spas today is on fresh, healthy foods that are prepared in innovative and appealing ways. They use ingredients that offer the most taste with the most nutritional punch. Sauces, rather than being excluded, are rethought so that the reliance on butter and cream is eliminated, and fresh fruits, vegetables, grains, and rich broths are taking the place formerly reserved for cream sauce and hollandaise.

Cooking for an Assisted-Living Center

Throughout the country, more and more people are moving into assisted-living centers. The level of assistance can vary greatly, but one of the popular features at any facility is food service. Although

this type of food has often been the butt of culinary jokes, the fact is that the centers are starting to fill up with baby boomers who are used to a certain lifestyle. Many of them may already be committed to a healthy lifestyle that includes plenty of good food and exercise. Of course, as they age, their lifestyles often need to morph a little to include dealing with the diseases that concern the aging, as well as the physical changes that can have an impact on their eating behaviors.

Summary

Cooking styles are changing drastically as we move forward into a new era of increasing awareness of the ways food and health are intertwined. The talented chef can chart his or her own way into some fascinating new opportunities.

In this area, even more than in some others, it is essential to keep abreast of new findings. Remember that nutrition is simply the study of how the body uses the food that it consumes. And remember that someone has to buy that food and cook that food before it gets eaten. That someone could be you. You might find that this is one of the most stimulating areas of the entire culinary field.

8

Volume Cooking

Cooking for institutions such as school cafeterias, day care centers, airlines, or jails is a career path that many people overlook. The word "institutional" may not have exactly the right connotation for them. However, working in volume or institutional feeding can be every bit as challenging, creative, and rewarding as working in a white tablecloth restaurant.

This chapter will look at the different types of work available in volume feeding, and the advantages to working for institutions such as hospitals and schools. They are substantial, and depending upon your own needs and the needs of your family, they could be the answer to a lot of concerns you might have.

What Is Volume Cooking?

There are distinct advantages to working in institutional feeding. Most often, your hours will be regular, and you will very likely not have to work on weekends or holidays. School cafeterias, for

instance, usually close during winter, spring, and summer breaks. The opportunity to learn additional skills is readily available; for example, you may be able to learn about purchasing for large organizations, which could eventually lead to an excellent position as steward or purchasing agent for a school, hospital, or other institution.

Finally—and this is the advantage that often catches the eye of many people—larger organizations can afford to offer their employees a very appealing benefits package, which may include paid vacations, sick days, personal time, medical and dental insurance, life insurance, and even profit-sharing. These benefits are not always possible in smaller operations. If you have a family, compare the cost of life and health insurance if you had to get it on your own.

Volume feeding is done in a wide variety of settings, and the volume can range from a few hundred to several thousand. The following are some of the avenues open to those pursuing a career in volume or institutional feeding.

Schools, Colleges, and Universities

Most schools have some sort of on-site cafeteria. Larger schools, colleges, and universities may have a variety of food service operations on campus, including a traditional cafeteria, a fast-food-style restaurant, a coffee shop, or other options.

Very often a large organization that handles the food service operation of several schools will be in charge. In that case, the managers will have received training from the parent organization. (The ARAMARK, formerly known as the Automated Retail Association, is one such organization that operates nationwide.)

guests of nursing homes are wholesome, nutritious, and interesting. There is also a special satisfaction for those people who care enough for the elderly or invalids to make their mealtimes delicious and satisfying.

Armed Forces

A large number of people who have entered the food service industry in the private business sector have done so after learning their skills in the armed forces. "Mess halls" aren't the only dining options, and it is more than possible to learn a great deal about food preparation, even food preparation of the highest caliber, in the armed forces.

The range of work in the armed forces for kitchen personnel is identical to what might be in a very large, very well-organized hotel chain. There are executive chefs, chefs, sous-chefs, line cooks, pantry cooks, and bakers.

Correctional Centers

City, county, state, and federal prisons have to feed their inmates. They have a responsibility, on a human level, to the prisoners to ensure that their physical needs of clothing, shelter, and food are supplied. They have an equal obligation to the taxpayers who must finance penal institutions to try to keep their efforts within a specified budget.

The challenge for the director of the food service operation is to make sure that three wholesome meals are served each day. It is important to learn how to get and use surplus items available through government programs, how to buy in bulk, and how to produce large amounts of food quickly and efficiently. This type of work is not for everyone, but it can be a rewarding job for some.

Contract Feeding

Many companies either operate cafeterias for their employees or contract with lunch wagons to come to the work site during coffee breaks and lunch hours for the convenience of their employees. They also find it more efficient to be able to keep their employees close to work during the day.

The size and general working philosophy of the company will determine how much or little it expects from a contract feeding service. Since the employees will be paying for their meals, it is, of course, important that the food be appealing enough that they will elect to buy it, rather than bring their own food or leave work at lunchtime.

Lunch wagons are often owned by one person who determines what kind of food and how much of it to prepare. There is a definite profit potential for the operators of these wagons. The hours can be long, but the rewards are usually ample.

There are a number of regulations that must be met to operate such a business, and it is very important that you understand all the laws governing it. You will need permits, inspections, and perhaps special insurance. Make sure that you fully investigate all the requirements first.

Airlines

Except for hospitals, airline food has one of the worst reputations going. This may be justified in some cases, but it certainly is not automatically true. Airlines are a business, and they need to remain competitive to attract business. People want good, hot food, whether they are on the ground or in the air. Consumers are demanding—and getting—better food on airplanes.

The food service operations, such as Marriott, that hold the contracts to prepare the food for airlines must perform what might sound like a miracle. In short, large quantities of food must be properly prepared, portioned, and packaged to fit into a specified amount of space and require no additional preparation apart from heating. Definitely challenging and exciting work!

Summary

Institutional feeding is far more exciting than you might at first think. Perhaps what puts people off initially is the unfortunate title of "institutional." But many people consider themselves very fortunate indeed to have found a job that allows them to work in the culinary arts while still having the time to live a normal family life.

Hospitals, schools, nursing homes, and airlines may not have the same glamour factor that a three-star white tablecloth restaurant has, but the fundamental work is the same: to provide good, fresh, wholesome food to the guest, whoever and wherever the guest is.

9

RESEARCH AND DEVELOPMENT

MANY PEOPLE HAVE exciting jobs working for groups that at first glance might not look like they would employ chefs. These groups include special interest organizations, research groups, manufacturers, and others.

Any company that produces a piece of equipment that is used in a kitchen, or a bottled sauce, spice, herb, or mustard, would like to be able to help a potential customer get the most out of its product. This is important if the company is to build consumer confidence, increase repeat business, and get to or stay at the top of the heap. Who better than a chef or someone trained in the culinary arts to help devise recipes, uses, videotapes, booklets, pamphlets, and cookbooks that promote the product?

The other area that we will look at in this chapter includes test kitchens operated by magazines, and paid recipe testers who assist in testing the recipes to be used in cookbooks.

Food Products Testers

Walk down any supermarket aisle and you are bombarded with a wide range of colorful and enticing packaged food products, all competing for your attention and money. Each product is carefully designed and packaged to appeal to you in some way—to your senses, your pocketbook, or even your conscience. The person who masterminds many of those decisions is a product developer who is part of a team that analyzes market trends, identifies a need, and develops products to meet those needs.

Food products testers are people who are responsible for developing, testing, and promoting food products. Typically, they have training in the basic sciences with an emphasis on foods. Workers in this occupation run laboratory tests on all kinds of prepared foods. What these tests are and how they will be conducted vary from product to product and among various processing methods. A few of the job duties of those working in this field include:

- Determining the chemical makeup of foods
- Testing a variety of mixes to make sure that they meet quality standards
- Recording amounts and kinds of ingredients present in the product
- Evaluating prepared food products by taste and aroma
- Evaluating texture, appearance, flavor, and nutritional value of food products
- Testing samples to ensure the safety of products
- Testing new recipes, suggesting new products, and promoting use of the product
- Verifying that products meet standard weights and measurements

Food products testers generally work a standard forty-hour week; however, those who work in seasonal processing industries may be required to work longer hours during the peak season.

To be successful in this area, you should receive specialized training in food technology. Research your local two- and four-year college to find courses in food science, since much of the work of the food products tester involves lab analysis. High school students who are interested in this field should prepare by taking mathematics, algebra, biology, English, and commercial food courses. College courses include food chemistry, food analysis, food microbiology, food engineering, food processing, physics, biology, and chemistry.

Corporate Research and Development

Companies that produce food products (General Foods, Pillsbury, and Heinz, for example) are constantly looking for new items that will capture the interest of the buying public. Before a new cereal, frozen food, cake mix, or salad dressing is introduced, it will undergo exhaustive evaluation and research, not only to determine its potential to make money, but also to find out how it acts when it is heated, refrigerated, stored on a shelf, or frozen.

The development of a new product or line of products for a food company usually falls into distinct phases. In the first phase, chefs prepare prototypes that are critically evaluated by every member of the team, including not only those responsible for developing a formula that can be manufactured efficiently but also those responsible for promoting and selling the item. Some of these items will move on for further testing to see how the target market for the product reacts to it. During this stage, chefs in research and development kitchens may be called upon to work out many refinements or adaptations to the original formula.

Promising new products or lines usually need careful development before they can go into production. Recipes, more likely called formulas, are worked out to account for issues of large volume production and quality control. Specific plans showing how the food is received and handled at all stages of manufacture are prepared and reviewed for adherence to all local and federal standards for food safety. The packaging and labeling details are also prepared and reviewed for accuracy and consistency with federal labeling language.

Preparing all the reports necessary for these important components usually falls to the research and development kitchen. In addition to the culinary skills required to create recipes or come up with ideas for food products, those who work in research and development departments or kitchens typically have a background in science and often have advanced degrees in fields related to food science. Incredible culinary technique may not be an absolute prerequisite for some of the more technical aspects of getting a food from idea into packaged, labeled item sitting on a grocery store shelf. But what is important is a commitment to quality and customer satisfaction—the very same commitment that is the primary focus of every practicing culinary professional.

Culinarians with a bent toward a more direct involvement with food and how it works in our bodies may spend their careers working with food in ways that most chefs would never consider to unlock the vast stores of information foods hold. Advances in our understanding of food safety, the ways foods can help or harm us, and the way foods grow and how they behave when stored or cooked have a direct bearing on everyone's quality of life. Programs such as NASA may not seem to have a direct relationship to the food service industry, but the work done for that agency resulted in the development of a hazard assessment system for food handlers known as HACCP (Hazard Analysis Critical Control Point), which helps to be certain that foods stay safe. Another example is the Centers for Disease Control in Atlanta, where culinary sleuths examine the origins and spread of food-borne illness outbreaks. Although these jobs certainly demand education and training in areas like biology, chemistry, and food science, the bottom line even here remains that it's all about the food we eat.

Working in Test Kitchens and Freelance Recipe Work

A test kitchen may be used for research and development, but test kitchens associated with magazines and newspapers are more likely to devote themselves to preparing written recipes intended for publication. The recipes are thoroughly tested to make sure that they work exactly as they are written. For some recipes, this might mean making the recipe several times over. Testers are expected to take note of cooking times, weights, volumes, temperatures, and consistencies. They also need to have a good understanding of how foods are supposed to look and taste when they are done.

A test kitchen, whether it is maintained by a company or a publication or is the home kitchen used by a freelancer, must be outfitted with equipment similar to that the ultimate consumer will use. For the home cook, then, you might find a facility outfitted with standard, household-sized stoves, pots, and pans. But if you are working for a publication that caters to the professional reader, there will be professional-scale-and-caliber equipment on hand.

Because there are significant expenses associated with maintaining and staffing an on-site test kitchen, many publications or companies rely upon freelance recipe developers and testers. Finding work in this area requires the same skills and tasks any freelancer needs to use: researching your market, networking, and doing the best job you possibly can on each and every assignment.

Freelance testers are often paid a flat fee for the development or testing of a recipe. These recipes are protected by copyright laws and are usually the property of the person or company hiring you to do the work. There are many types of testing that a recipe might require.

Individuals who thrive at this kind of work are detail-oriented, good at observation, excellent communicators, and good cooks. They often work for magazine editors or cookbook authors, councils or advisory boards, companies that manufacture or produce ingredients or tools for the kitchen, and food-related websites.

Magazines

Magazines devoted to writing about food often incorporate recipes as well. The person writing about a particular food needs to have the ability not only to write and do research, but also to develop recipes that will showcase the special flavor, texture, color, or nutritional characteristic of a food to its best advantage. This means that the person doing the writing must be able to organize a body of research and put it into a context that the home or professional cook can make use of.

As there is increasing interest in special foods, such as farm-raised game animals or organic produce, there is increasing demand to know how to choose the best quality item from among the oftentimes bewildering range of selections. Technological advances also are responsible for increasing the number of options available to the chef and the home cook.

The work done in the test kitchens of magazines can be among the most fascinating that a food writer can find. It combines the best of both worlds: working with food and then writing about it. In many cases, this work also may offer an opportunity to break into the world of food styling and even food photography.

Cookbooks

The number of cookbooks being published each year is staggering. And one of the most time-consuming parts of writing any cookbook or cooking articles is testing the recipes.

Authors and editors often hire freelance testers to check the recipes. They want to know if the measurements given will produce a dish that is appealing, tasty, and attractive. They also want to know if the recipes can be easily understood. If and when you land a contract to write your own cookbook, you will be the one responsible for seeing that the recipe testing is done correctly.

If you don't happen to know any cookbook editors or authors personally, you can try to break into this work by writing directly to the publications or authors using what is known as a query letter. Such a letter describes the recipes you might develop for an issue or gives information about the types of recipe development that you have already done.

Recipe testers are often paid a flat fee per recipe, in addition to being reimbursed for the food items purchased to prepare the recipes.

Promotional Boards and Advertising Agencies

When you buy a box of cornmeal and see that there are recipes on the back of the box, do you ever wonder where those recipes come from? And when you get a small pamphlet of recipes from a cocoa producer, do you know where those recipes were developed?

There are many organizations, such as the National Avocado Advisory or the Potato Council, that have newsletters that are sent to the trade or to consumers to help build interest in certain products. Of particular importance to these publications are their recipes, which act as a blueprint to get the consumer to try the product, whether it is a new and unfamiliar product or an old standard that needs a face-lift. Although staff members working in an on-site test kitchen may write some of these recipes, many more rely upon freelance workers.

Equipment Manufacturers

Practically every cooking appliance, whether it is large or small, arrives in its box along with a recipe booklet that includes detailed instructions for operating the equipment and producing a variety of dishes using the equipment. These recipes are developed and carefully tested to make sure that the consumer will be able to understand them and make them work.

This type of work can take a good deal of time and effort, but it can be exciting, too. You might have an opportunity to work with tools not yet available to the public and either produce informative manuals or instruct consumers in the tools' safe and efficient use. In addition, you might be called upon to develop recipes that show off the versatility and functionality of the tools. There is, as yet, no specific course of study suggested for this kind of work. These manuals and recipes demand clear and explicit communication skills, whether you are taking notes, preparing reports, writing step-by-step directions for assembling a tool, or writing a recipe.

Nutritional Menu and Product Development

Continued work on the part of nutritionists is opening the doors to an onrush of interest in cooking that is based on grains and legumes and fresh vegetables and fish, rather than on the traditional "American" high-protein, high-fat diet. Nutritionists are the catalysts for this new information. But unless and until a chef is available to take these practical concerns and translate them into a meal that satisfies on several levels—taste, satiety, texture, and general appeal—then it is not possible for the average chef to make use of these new pieces of information. Instead he or she will be inclined to stick to the tried-and-true recipes that are sure to please customers.

When restaurants or food processors try to make changes that are aimed at improving nutrition, they often need help to develop recipes and techniques suitable for their specific operations.

Today, this often means finding intriguing new recipes drawn from a host of exciting cuisines. They may include elements that need to be refined for use in a volume-production setting. Developing recipes and formulas for new menu items may be the task of a consultant able to synthesize nutrition and culinary information into menu items that sell well and turn a profit.

Summary

The type of work available in the field of research and development can be extremely exciting. Many of the opportunities outlined above are the domain of freelance researchers and testers. If you are flexible and if you prefer to work on a freelance basis, you can find great numbers of opportunities. Very often the work that companies, individuals, or groups need is on a project-by-project basis. It can be a challenge to keep your workload and your income consistent, but many people find that the trade-offs, like having control over their schedules and workload and the ability to choose among interesting projects, are adequate reward.

A career as a researcher devoted to food and cooking usually sets an individual on the path to higher education, often culminating in a doctoral degree. For people involved with research in the areas of health, nutrition, and manufacturing, work is more often to be found with colleges, universities, and established research facilities run either by the federal government or large corporations.

10

Running Your Own Business

Many people hold a special dream. They want to own their own business someday. They want to be in charge and do the work the right way, which is to say their own way. With every job they have, they tuck away ideas about what they would or wouldn't do if they only had their own place.

This chapter will look at some of the types of operations people own or are the managers of for larger groups. This work takes a very special kind of personality. You have to have a great deal of self-motivation as well as greater reserves of stamina, endurance, and money than you might have originally thought necessary.

In addition to careers that will have you in the kitchen working with food on a day-to-day basis, there are other avenues that can be taken. Many people find that as their lives and interests change, they are ready to move from a position in the kitchen, no matter how responsible, to management of an operation, whether it is as the manager in a large hotel or as the owner of a business.

Of all the challenges that you may face, owning your own establishment is certainly one of the greatest. And though many people dream of having their own bistro, restaurant, bed and breakfast, or hotel, it is much more difficult to achieve this goal than most people can ever guess. In addition to these more traditional operations, there are a number of other businesses that you can go into for yourself that are worth considering, if that is your inclination.

Food and Beverage Manager

This is a position that many in the culinary field are headed for. They make careful decisions regarding the type of education they will receive and where they will receive it. Managing an operation is a job that requires many talents. In the past, there was a great gulf perceived between chefs and food and beverage managers. But these days, as more and more people move from the kitchen into management, the overall operation of a hotel almost invariably benefits.

Graduates with management degrees very often spend some time looking at how the restaurant operation affects overall operation, but they do not have a good feeling for what is actually possible in a particular kitchen or in a certain type of dining room. As a result, there can be some loss of efficiency. The chef turned manager, however, knows very well what the kitchen or dining room can accomplish. Consequently, he or she can offer many skills that someone trained solely in the management of a business cannot.

Your Own Restaurant

This is the dream of a lifetime for many people. And those who have managed to achieve this dream will be the first to say that their dreams did not come anywhere near the reality of dealing with the day-to-day drama of restaurant operation.

Whether you are the proud owner of a small bistro or a large steak house, you will find that even more than as an employee you are at the mercy of the paying public. No one can accurately predict what will work and what will not. There is simply no guarantee that the restaurant will be a success, and the rate of failure for restaurants is incredibly high.

Before going into business for yourself, you should try to give yourself every possible advantage. Do a market analysis to find out if there is a potential market for the cuisine you would like to offer. Talk to other business owners in the area and try to get a feel for when business might be good, and when it might slow down. Consider your location carefully. Is it easily accessible, or will your guests get lost on the way to your door? Can they park once they get there? What is the neighborhood like?

Have someone you trust look over the building you are about to buy, or have them watch over the construction of a new building. There are so many potential problems here that it is impossible to begin to list them all. But be aware that things can go wrong, and they do go wrong. You and your partners, if any, should plan to spend more money on getting the business ready to open than you ever dreamed.

Learn about the permits, licenses, and inspections you will need to have done. Your business will affect the surrounding area, and you may have something in mind for your restaurant that is not permitted according to the current zoning ordinance. Before you build a patio and order umbrellas, find out if outside seating is allowed.

Getting all of this information together will take time and money. Look at it as an investment in your future and in the future of your business. And remember that even with as much research as you can manage to do, turning every possible stone and reading every possible code, there will be unpredictable events. You could be open for a month, only to lose your power for a week due to an untimely blizzard. Or your air-conditioning could blow out during one of the hottest weeks of the entire year.

The owner of a restaurant is the person who works the hardest weeks and the longest days. He or she has to deal with wait staff, bartenders, purveyors, kitchen staff, and dishwashers. He or she is the one who has to find enough champagne glasses for a wedding party. But, he or she is also the one who garners the greatest benefit and the most satisfaction from the restaurant.

Bed-and-Breakfast

For many people, especially couples, this is an ideal compromise. You need a large home with at least one extra bedroom, and a place to serve breakfast to your guests. With those minimal requirements met, you can open a bed-and-breakfast.

There are several distinct advantages to running a bed-and-breakfast. You can determine when you will be open. If there is a time of year when you don't wish to work, you simply don't take any reservations. Breakfast is traditionally the only meal that is served, so once that meal has been taken care of, the rest of the operation would revolve around housekeeping chores—cleaning rooms and baths, changing linens, and bookkeeping chores.

Occasionally a bed-and-breakfast will decide to offer limited dining service. Guests staying at the bed-and-breakfast, and in some cases other customers, will make a reservation for dinner. Quite often there is a set menu with fixed seating. In this way, the chef can plan very accurately how much food to prepare, and the workload can be scheduled to make the best use of everyone's time.

The disadvantage is that you will have strangers in your home. This is a situation that is easier for some people to deal with than others. If you are a very private person, you may want to consider carefully how you would feel to have strangers walking through the rooms of your home, perusing your bookshelves, and admiring family photographs.

Lunch Wagons and Lunch Stands

We have all seen those trucks that are parked by the side of the road, or the carts that line the streets of most cities. The foods they offer can range from hot dogs with "the works" to more exotic items such as kebabs, croissants, and even Creole dishes. In fact, there is practically no limit to the kinds of foods that street vendors are able to produce and sell from their trucks or carts.

The earning potential for this kind of business is higher than you might imagine. Some people work only part of the year and use their earnings to spend the remaining months on vacation or living at their second home. Don't write this off as a means to be in business for yourself. Some people eventually run a fleet of lunch wagons. In a society that does more things on the run than it ever did before, a service that is on your way to the gym or that comes directly to your work site is a great boon.

Each town and city has different regulations governing how many lunch trucks there can be, where they can be located, and other considerations. Be sure to find out all the small details before you invest in the wagon. And do plenty of research on traffic patterns, what people normally do on their way to work, and what they do during their lunch hours before you select your territory.

Private Catering

This is another way to get into business with a limited amount of capital and low overhead expenses. Many people work out of their homes, providing food for other people's dinner parties, cocktail parties, receptions, baptisms, showers, and the myriad other events that call for a celebration with food.

One word of caution, however. There are health regulations that must be observed. If you are transporting prepared food, you will need a way to ensure that it is kept within the correct temperature range. You also may have to undergo an inspection of your kitchen to make sure that it is safe.

This can be an extremely exciting business, and again, like bed-and-breakfasts, it is one that you can tailor to suit your own schedule. If you know that you want to take a vacation with your family in mid-March, you simply don't take on any parties at that time.

The area of the country in which you live also will have a direct influence on how busy you are and the kind of parties you will be able to find. Entertaining does happen in waves. The summer months are usually very busy, as are the months around the Christmas and Hanukkah holidays. But there may be other busy times of the year in other areas. Try to find out as much as you can before placing an ad in the local newspaper.

Catering Small Affairs

There are many different styles for caterers. Some people handle only small affairs that are catered directly in people's homes. They may impose a ceiling of no more than fifty guests, for example. This means that they are able to keep down the number of employees they need to help wait tables, prepare food, and tend bar.

Catering Large Affairs

Other caterers like to handle larger affairs ranging from one hundred people to one thousand or more. These large events take a great deal of strategy and planning, and usually there are fewer events of this size throughout the year. It becomes increasingly important to have a readily available source of temporary staff. If you are located in an area with a college then you are probably in luck.

Catering Office Affairs

Another type of catering is geared directly to offices. You can offer a special service to offices. The way it works is this: you establish a contact in an office building and distribute a menu. The orders are placed by a specified time, and you prepare and deliver the food at a specified time as well. The type of menu that you offer can be as diverse or as simple as you believe you can handle. However, remember to give careful thought to how you will package and deliver the food before you branch out to too many offices. Cold food that should be hot and leaky brown paper bags do little to enhance your image. In addition to lunches, some caterers offer services that will provide foods for coffee breaks in the morning and afternoon.

Summary

No matter what the size of your business, the challenges are great and the rewards can be equally great.

There are obviously a number of different types of businesses that were not mentioned here. They may have been touched on briefly in another chapter, or they may simply still be stashed away in the fertile imagination of someone who is reading this book. The chances are there; if you have courage, luck, and determination, you can make something out of them.

11

WHERE ELSE DOES CULINARY CREATIVITY THRIVE?

THERE ARE SEVERAL careers that work directly with food that are not actually involved in preparing foods to be eaten by a paying public. Photographers, stylists, and writers are all important to the food service industry in a number of ways. They are a central clearinghouse for new ideas, they help establish and demolish trends, and they set the standards by which the public judges what happens in restaurants. There are also fascinating positions in sales and service, public relations, advertising, and media.

Food Photography and Styling

Have you ever picked up a magazine or a book simply because the food on the front cover looked so appealing that you wanted to eat it? It takes someone with a very special talent to produce pictures of such breathtaking beauty and style. It isn't always easy to make food look appealing in a photograph.

When the food is sitting right in front of you, your senses of smell and taste will have an influence on how appealing (or unappealing) it is. You can experience the different textures, the temperature, the thickness, and the spiciness—all of the elements that are so important. But with photography, you have only your vision to go on.

Some foods are not visually appealing. But the challenge is somehow to make them look that way, whether the photo is for an ad campaign, a feature story in a magazine, or the front cover of a new cookbook.

There is really no school as such that specializes in food photography, although there are courses that you can take. It is important to understand the basic principles of photography and lighting, how to operate a camera, and how to arrange foods so that they look appealing.

Food Styling

The preparation of the food being photographed and the way it is placed or arranged is often the work of a second person, known as a food stylist. When you look at a magazine article and are struck by the way the food is spread out on a plate or the way it is garnished or the presence or lack of other items in the photograph, it is usually the work of the food stylist you are reacting to. Like food photographers, food stylists undergo primarily on-the-job training. There are a few courses that you can take, but in general, it is not something in which you can major at college.

It is up to the stylist to make sure that the lettuce leaves are perfect, with not a single detectable fault, and that the sauce is carefully ladled onto the plate after the chicken is arranged to achieve the greatest impact.

Without some knowledge of food—how to select the best product and apply the right technique, how to cut the vegetables and slice the turkey—the stylist would be at a loss.

Food Writing and Communications

All you have to do is walk into any bookstore to see that there is a large, and seemingly inexhaustible, market for cookbooks. They range from single-subject books on anything from beans to chocolate to books that center on a particular type of cuisine or ethnic style. There also are books that are encyclopedic in their scope.

The people who write and edit these books have to have a good basic knowledge of food and cooking for these books to work. And writing books is just one avenue for the person who wants to write about food.

Restaurant Critics

Restaurant critics are as important to restaurants as the people who will dine in them. It is certainly true that critics are notorious for their highly personalized opinions, but it is interesting to note just how influential some critics can be. This kind of writing job is not easy to come by, and the people who hold these highly coveted positions often cultivate an aura of glamour and mystery. Fundamentally, however, if a reviewer is to be taken seriously, he or she needs to have a solid grounding in what constitutes both good food and good cooking. In addition, he or she also should be able to discuss the wine list, the style of the restaurant, and trends in the restaurant business.

Writing for Trade and Consumer Publications

There are many trade and consumer publications that focus on food, and many newspapers devote a portion of their papers (usually on Wednesday) to food and entertainment. The person who writes these articles is usually well read in the culinary arts and proficient in the kitchen as well. The kinds of articles that might be called for could range from a simple discussion of how to brew a pot of tea to an informational piece on nutritional cooking or special new foods.

Reviews of cookbooks, small pieces on new foods or equipment, human interest stories, press releases—all of these are examples of the kinds of pieces that you may be able to pitch to magazines to start your portfolio. Read the publications, both trade and consumer, to see what their audiences are like. There are special publications that will explain how to submit articles to magazines for consideration.

Writing Copy

When the holidays come around, practically everyone with a mailbox is deluged with catalogs that offer foods that run the gamut from cheese baskets to fruits of the month, smoked sturgeon to imported beluga caviar. Deciding what kinds of foods to include in the catalog, and how to describe them, could be a fascinating job for someone who loves good food.

The number of companies that produce or sell food items or equipment for preparing foods, the national councils that promote a particular food, and other special-interest groups that are directly or indirectly related to the culinary arts is staggering the first time you find out about them. Who would have imagined a National Cling Peach Advisory Board? But there are such organizations, and countless others. Some have been around a long time, like the National Dairy Council, while others are relatively young.

What they all have in common is that they need people to help them get their message to the public. This may mean that they need writers, photographers, and stylists, and people to develop recipes that showcase their products or equipment. The smaller the operation, the more likely it is that you might be called upon to do a number of these jobs.

In fact, these jobs can be a wonderful training ground if you have your heart set on the more glamorous heights that were discussed earlier in this chapter.

There also are numerous advertising agencies, some of which handle food and food-related clients exclusively. The campaigns that these companies devise for their clients are often incredibly innovative and exciting. And someone who knows about food has had a big hand in getting these campaigns off the ground, from helping to develop the original concept to getting the food onto the plate and into the photo.

It may be helpful to take additional courses in marketing and advertising to qualify for the jobs that really appeal to you, but experience on the job is something that is worth its weight in gold.

Getting Experience

The way to break into food writing is simply to write as much as you can and try to get your work published wherever you can. Small local papers are always looking for someone to write for them; the catch is that they will probably not pay much, if they can pay anything at all. You will have the chance to have your work published, though. Don't forget you have to pay your dues if you want to break into this field.

Another way to get some experience is to help with organizations that want to put together small cookbooks as a money-raising project. Junior League books are increasingly sophisticated, as are other cookbooks sponsored by church and town organizations. The practice of writing and editing recipes can be invaluable. If nothing else, you will find out immediately if this is something that you can do on a day-in and day-out basis.

Being able to hold a published piece that you have written or helped to write in your hand is the same as holding a diploma. However, it can take a long time to get to that point, so don't be discouraged if you truly want to write about food.

Sales

As cooking styles from around the world become more widespread and familiar, chefs look for a whole bevy of new products, such as ingredients, tools, or serving pieces, to keep their menus lively and their bottom line healthy. Someone trained and with a background in the food service industry has a distinct advantage. Whether you work for a large purveyor or you are a sales force of one for your artisanal cheeses, you have a base of knowledge that can give you an edge. For instance, you would never show up to peddle your wares at 12:30 P.M. on Tuesday at a restaurant that is most famous for its lunches. Sales jobs demand great communication skills, especially verbal communication, in a one-on-one setting. Organization, attention to detail, punctuality, and honesty are also found on the résumé of the skilled and successful salesperson.

Media

Earlier in this book we talked about the chef as a star, but that star is not alone. There are many people behind the scenes working diligently to make sure that this star stays bright. These workers may handle the chef's public relations or write speeches, scripts, and presentations. They may be the ones required to order food and hire staff for a cooking demonstration or competition. Among the many types of work in the big world of media, you can find a fit for your culinary skills and inclinations along with your other skills, whether they are in the area of communication, development, fund-raising, or technology.

Summary

Magazines, advertisements, videos, and photographs of food are of seemingly endless interest to the American public. What makes them work is the level of expertise it took to produce them.

If the public is confident that the person who is writing about a restaurant could actually cook a meal, or that the video about preparing fish or cooking healthy food has been written by someone who truly does understand the material that is covered in it, then it works. And the way this happens is to have someone involved who can cook, who loves food, and who understands what is happening when you apply heat to foods.

12

GETTING A START AND
MOVING AHEAD

To GET A good job, get a good education. There is no substitute for experience, and there is no substitute for education. The type of education and training that will serve well in your career in the culinary arts is not exactly similar to what it might be for other fields. Rather than spending long hours in a library, learning the theories and concepts behind a particular body of work, the chef-in-training needs an education that incorporates a large degree of hands-on, practical work.

There are different approaches to getting this education, but it is the responsibility of cooking students to make sure that the training they undertake is of a type that is directly suited to whatever future goals they may have.

If, for instance, you have a burning desire to work with a magazine as its food stylist or photographer, knowing how to handle food and how to recognize what is the best appearance or quality of an item is invaluable. So, too, is the knowledge of how to use lighting, how to frame a picture, and how to arrange food in such a way that, with the benefit of only sight, it appeals not only to the eye but also to the senses of touch, taste, and smell.

If your goal is to work in consultation, helping people to develop and maintain nutritious diets, not only do you need to know how to broil, bake, roast, and steam foods, you also need to understand how the body uses food to maintain itself. Further studies in nutrition, as well as biology and chemistry, are essential.

Chefs who hope to one day own and operate their own businesses need fundamental information about basic business operation, accounting, and marketing. Some elementary knowledge about the law is important, too. Learning how to deal with people who will be working for you is another area to consider. Whether you approach this aspect of your job by reading the many books, manuals, and articles available or by attending classes, seminars, or workshops, this sort of training can be invaluable.

But first, if you want to work in the culinary arts, you need to know how to cook. Cooking is something that can be learned. Proficiency at the craft is something attained through practice and continued study. Excellence is something that is achieved over the course of a life's work. It is important to remember that there is always something better, something more nearly perfect than anything you may have accomplished. There is always more to learn; you should never stop until you hang up your apron and put away your knives for good.

Is Culinary School Right for You?

There is a growing number of excellent cooking schools in the United States and Canada. As the food service industry continues to expand, the demand for skilled workers is going to increase as well. Jobs for chefs and others in the food service industry are projected to grow at rates between 20 and 45 percent by the year 2006. The number of schools available to train these workers will need to increase to meet this kind of demand. And the skills that they will be teaching their students will change as well.

Cooking schools vary in a number of ways. Some are fully accredited colleges and universities devoted solely to the culinary arts, such as the Culinary Institute of America or the Baltimore Culinary Academy. Other culinary schools may be part of a larger college or university, such as Johnson and Wales. There are programs available in community colleges, technical schools, and through adult education programs offered by local school districts. Some may lead to a certificate or a diploma.

There are short programs, lasting only six to eight weeks or perhaps three months. These classes may cover one technique or style of cooking. Others may offer a more complete course of study that lasts from two to four years, culminating in a degree such as an Associate of Occupational Science (A.O.S.) or a Bachelor of Science or of Professional Studies (B.S. or B.P.S.). The type of training you decide on should take into account how the training will meet your needs.

If you are just starting out and want to discover if a career in the culinary arts is something you really want, a short course at a vocational or technical school may be just the ticket. That, coupled with a job in a restaurant or hotel kitchen, should give you an indication of whether the work, the hours, and the service field in general are for you.

If you have had additional experience, or if you are quite sure this is the field you want to be in, a more comprehensive educational experience is what you should aim for. The following considerations should help you determine whether a school will meet your needs.

Faculty

How many faculty members are there? Some schools may offer only a large demonstration kitchen with many students watching as a chef prepares food and gives lectures. Other schools have a larger faculty and a number of kitchens, where students actually work with the food and have ready access to a chef/instructor.

Ask if you can tour the school and see how the classes are run and how big they are. It is extremely difficult to learn to cook well without getting your own hands on the food—cutting it, sautéing it, plating it, and serving it. It is one thing to read about making a hollandaise sauce and quite another to actually make it.

Small classes—where everyone has a chance to ask questions and try a technique—are the ideal. The more students an instructor has to deal with, the less likely you are to get a good education.

Facilities

Does the school have enough kitchens and enough equipment in those kitchens to give you a well-rounded education? It isn't enough to know how to boil a vegetable and pan-fry a piece of chicken. As you progress in your career, you will be called upon to perform a number of different tasks, from making a stock or soup to preparing a delicate sauce to baking elegant pastries.

There should be at least enough pots and pans for everyone in the class to have a hands-on experience. Look around to see if there are conventional and convection ovens, grills, broilers, large worktables, and enough refrigeration space.

If the school operates its own restaurant, try to eat there. The menu will give you some idea of how contemporary its style of cooking is and what type of facilities it has. Pastries and breads require a bakeshop. Cutting meats may require a butcher shop. Ask about the menu items and how they are prepared.

There are also times when a lecture is the most effective learning tool. Are there lecture rooms, audiovisual equipment, and desks available? Is there a library? Most people are surprised at how much reading and research the truly dedicated chef does. It is never enough to simply sit back and do it the same way because "this is the way it has always been done." There are new products, unfamiliar foods, exciting new ways to present foods, and flavor combinations that can change the way you understand cooking. It is important to learn how to learn about food.

Are the facilities clean and well-lit? These are not "the olden days," and kitchens are no longer synonymous with dungeons. The walls, vents, and hoods should show no evidence of grease and dirt having been allowed to build up. There shouldn't be any cracks and holes in the walls. Refrigerators should be operating at the correct temperature. Work areas should be well lit to ensure that the people using sharp knives work safely.

The care and pride taken in the school's kitchens and other facilities is indicative of how important the process of educating a student is to the school. You should be learning more than simply how to cook; you also should be learning how to keep a kitchen clean, safe, and running well.

Curriculum

How much time is actually spent cooking? After all, the craft (or art) you are trying to master is that of cooking.

There are fundamentals that have to be mastered before going on to more advanced work. In the same manner that it is essential to learn the basics of color and line if one wishes to become a graphic artist, or the basics of operating a camera to become a photographer, the chef must have complete mastery of techniques that apply to food: boiling, steaming, braising, stewing, roasting, grilling, sautéing, baking, and many others.

And even before attempting these techniques, other, more basic, concepts and skills must be mastered: recognizing quality (or lack thereof) in products; proper purchasing, storing, and handling techniques; ensuring the best-quality product as well as the ultimate safety and satisfaction of the guest. The proper care and use of a knife, the basic knife cuts, and certain fundamental preparations are important foundations to any culinary education.

You may decide that a four-year education leading to a bachelor's degree in hotel administration is best for you. But, if your real aim is to be the executive chef in charge of a kitchen, or a string of kitchens, that curriculum may not offer enough hands-on cooking experience. You may need to bolster the knowledge you would gain at a school such as Cornell with some additional time and training at a school like the Culinary Institute of America, or vice versa.

Accreditation

Your degree's value relates directly to the kind of accreditation the school has. To grant a degree or certificate, schools must meet certain standards established by the state and enforced by means of a rigorous application and review process. Not only does this matter in terms of the quality of education you are likely to receive, it also has a direct bearing upon the financial aid that is ultimately available to you.

Financial Aid

Since most students will need to finance their culinary education, a well-organized, committed, and up-to-date financial aid office is imperative. Good offices can offer a wide range of assistance to students, steering them to the most appropriate programs, helping them find their way in a maze of scholarship and grant offerings, and generally making their entire time at the college an easier and more productive experience.

Certification

Professional organizations devoted to the culinary and baking and pastry arts have a great deal of influence throughout the industry. By establishing professional standards and goals, as well as an effective way to measure how well chefs stack up against these standards, they have been able to create a more uniform way to recognize a culinarian's professional status. The distinctions of Certified Master Chef (C.M.C.), Certified Executive Chef (C.E.C.), Certified Culinary Educator (C.C.E.), and Certified Master Baker (C.M.B.) are just some of the levels awarded by such groups as the American Bakers Association and the American Culinary Federation (ACF).

These organizations have all created a ladder that members climb, starting at the apprentice or student level and eventually advancing to executive levels. This system owes its structure to medieval times, when craft guilds flourished. At that time, after serving a period of apprenticeship in a particular guild (there was one for large cuts of meat; one for poultry, pies, and tarts; one for sauces; and one for caterers who organized weddings and various meals served in personal homes), the apprentice had to create a masterpiece and pay a fee to each member of the organization. To be assured that a craftsperson—whether chef, blacksmith, or carpenter—had truly mastered the craft, it was necessary to go through several distinct and carefully controlled stages of learning.

The Apprenticeship System

Today, the apprentice system is still a highly respected means of acquiring a culinary education, albeit a less formal one than attending a culinary school. Even today it is not uncommon to hear about chefs who can trace their "lineage" through only two or three degrees of separation to the influence of Escoffier or Careme. Paul Bocuse, for example, perhaps one of the most renowned and revered chefs of this age, trained under Fernand Point, a disciple of Auguste Escoffier. Escoffier is the Frenchman responsible for developing and recording a style of cookery entirely new in both production and presentation.

In the first part of the apprenticeship, tasks are generally limited to peeling and preparing vegetables, preparing stocks, and keeping the kitchen clean. The rate at which the apprentice moves from these elementary tasks to those that are more demanding and challenging depends on two things. The first is the amount of energy and effort the apprentice puts into learning through observation, reading, and working extra hours to get more information. The second is the temperament of the chef.

Apprentices who work toward their accreditation in the ACF in the United States are required to take courses at a college during their training. This gives a broader perspective to the training received in the kitchen and results in a more well-rounded education that will pay off handsomely when it is time to look for a full-fledged job.

Finding Culinary Mentors

A formal education is, for most chefs, just the start of their careers. It is still highly desirable to spend some time training under a chef whose talents are respected, whose approach to cuisine is highly thought of, and whose food is not simply "a flash in the pan" but has withstood the test of time. Many cities throughout the United States and Canada boast world-class cuisine offered in cutting-edge restaurants. The first career move of many highly successful chefs, such as Todd English and Larry Forgione, is to find someone to work for who can teach you more about your craft. Sometimes this choice leads you away from more lucrative job offers or more exalted titles.

For many people it remains a dream to go to Europe and work there under some of the acknowledged masters of the craft. Before doing so be sure that you have done what you can to smooth the way. Try to have a job lined up and make sure that you have the proper letters of introduction. They can be enormously helpful. Another important thing to remember is that you must have working papers to work legally overseas. These papers are not always easy to arrange. Try to get your future employer to give you some assistance.

Launching Your Career

Experience is the best teacher. Without taking the knowledge gained in a school or through reading or through practicing at home and putting it to the test in a professional kitchen, your status will probably never be anything greater than that of a devoted amateur. And although there is a great deal to be said for perfecting one's hobbies, it is not really what you are after.

Formal education, though of great value, is not enough. And, in truth, it is quite possible to rise to the highest levels in this profession without ever once attending a school or taking a class. Formal training can mark the start of one's career or be an adjunct to a career that has already been started.

The people who have risen to the top without formal training have spent a great deal of time learning their craft in the crucible itself—directly in a professional kitchen. The training that is received in a working kitchen is invaluable, which is why many cooking schools do their best to simulate a restaurant as part of their curricula.

The experience of working in a hotel kitchen is quite different from that of working in a small French bistro. The ability to work well with fish is a different skill from that of sautéing meat. Ideally, you will have an opportunity to work in a number of different kitchens, positions, and capacities as you learn your craft, so that your career can be as rich, full, and rewarding as you deserve.

You may find that in a large kitchen, you will have the time to concentrate on a more specialized area of work. For instance, your work may be to butcher the meats. After breaking down several legs of veal, the procedure becomes increasingly simple. With continued practice, you learn speed and efficiency. You also will learn how to determine the quality of the meat by its color, the amount of fat it has, and the grain. This kind of learning can happen only through experience.

In a smaller kitchen, you will be called upon to use a broader range of skills. You may need to learn to fill out inventory sheets and work with purveyors, receive goods, cut meats, and prepare vegetables, sauces, and soups. All of these tasks will need to be accomplished prior to the time that guests begin to arrive. This requires a familiarity with the menu, the ability to organize, and the ability to set priorities.

As you continue through your career, all of your past work experiences should be brought to bear on the work you currently are doing. The ability to attend to a great number of details is just as important whether you are catering a banquet for five hundred or preparing twenty-five dinners each evening in a small restaurant; whether you need to oversee a large staff or manage only yourself, a staff of one.

There are countless lessons to be learned that only time will teach. Each job that you undertake will have its own set of challenges and rewards. The sum of your experiences is what will prove your ability in this career.

Keeping Your Career Alive

Those individuals who advance along a career path have usually exercised great vigilance to be sure they are not left behind. Today, a professional culinarian needs to know about food trends, advances in technology, new equipment and products, wine, art, history, popular culture (including movies, novels, magazines, and sports), and architecture. Travel is highly recommended, as is dining out frequently, to be sure that you are up to speed on the changes in the food service industry.

Reading

Reading is essential. You need to know what is going on in the world around you. The kitchen can be an all-consuming passion for some people, but without the broadening influence of the rest of the world, it can also make a person narrow to the point of shallowness. You have to make the effort to find those minutes during the day to read the newspaper. And more than reading the paper and listening to the news, you need to read books about whatever you enjoy, as well as those subjects that can help you in your work. At first glance, some of these subjects may not seem to have a lot to do with cooking: art, history, architecture, and science, for example. But they all contribute in some way to the development of your craft and your skills.

The success or failure of a restaurant, hotel, or any type of food service establishment depends completely upon whether you have customers. The paying public can be fickle, and there is no scientific way to ensure that any operation will be a success. Keeping in touch with what people want, the trends that are important, and the changes in lifestyle that affect your clientele are so important that this aspect of your work cannot be overstated.

Once a winning combination has been found, it is extremely difficult to bring yourself to change things. And that old adage, "If it ain't broke, don't fix it," applies more often than one might think. But, being aware of when things are starting to rattle a little is essential to your livelihood, whether it is your own operation that is under scrutiny or your career path. Fine-tuning and tinkering not only are acceptable but are encouraged. Keeping in touch with what the rest of the world is up to while you are working in the kitchen is the only way you can find out when you need a tune-up.

There are a number of journals, periodicals, and magazines aimed at both professionals and amateurs interested in the culinary arts. There is a tendency, on the one hand, to find the professional journals a little less glamorous than those aimed at the amateur and, on the other hand, to think that those aimed at the home cook may have nothing of value for a professional. Don't fall victim to either one of these traps.

Dining Out and Traveling

Go to other restaurants as often as you can. You need to know what other people are doing. What size portions do they offer? How do their sauces compare to yours? What size wine list do they have? Certainly going out to eat is a wonderful way to relax, but it is also an important way to build up contacts and find out about new products and services available.

Many of the trends that appear seemingly from nowhere, such as the craze for stir-frying or using wild mushrooms or spicy foods, can be traced to an adventurous and influential chef's trip to a different part of our own country or to a foreign country. We tend to become fond of the way things have always been done, but in a new environment, eating unfamiliar foods prepared in ways we are not accustomed to, we begin to see the possibilities of a spice or another ingredient that we may not have considered at home.

Networking

There is a strong network of people in the culinary arts. You are, or will be, a member of that network, too. Don't be shy; use the opportunities available to meet other chefs and restaurant owners, food writers, and photographers. You all have a common ground: the love of food.

One way to begin networking is simply to introduce yourself to the chef at a restaurant. Though this may seem like a presumptuous thing to do when you first try it, you will quickly learn that if you choose your time correctly—that is, not at the height of bedlam during service on a Saturday night—most chefs are anxious to meet other members of their profession.

Professional Organizations

Join professional organizations such as the American Culinary Federation, the National Restaurant Association, and other national and local organizations. And remember to get involved in local politics, national politics—anything that can affect your career.

These organizations usually publish newsletters or magazines that act as a forum for information and provide discussions on various concerns that affect people in the culinary arts. Very often they act as a powerful voice to address the lawmakers of the land and to serve as a way of focusing the energy and power of their membership.

Competitions and Salons

Food competitions, from local chili cook-offs to worldwide competition at the Culinary Olympics, are an invaluable means of sharpening and honing skills. Food preferences, styles of presentation, cooking techniques—all these have changed enormously in the last several years. They will no doubt continue to change in response to the creativity and drive of the new professionals arriving on the scene and to the ongoing development of personal styles by established chefs.

In addition to perfecting your own technique, competitions will introduce you to the work of others. You will have the opportunity to see how a food might look presented in a way you never thought of and that no magazine has ever depicted. In short, you will find yourself on the cutting edge of high-tech culinary arts.

Conferences and Conventions

Throughout the year, conference centers in cities throughout the land host conventions, expos, and conferences devoted to the restaurant industry. There are shows to introduce the latest thing in fancy foods. Others concentrate on equipment or china and table linens. As part of the event, there are often seminars and workshops that explore areas of particular interest to the food service industry, ranging from legal issues to cost management to trends and themes.

Planning for Five, Ten, and Fifteen Years

No one but you can determine where you'd like to be in the future. But it's a fairly sure bet that as you go out on interviews, someone is going to ask you. You should have an honest, well-thought-out answer ready.

Think about your goals and write them down. Don't be deterred by your current state of finances, experience, or education. Once you know where you'd like to go, you can get down to the business of planning the trip. On a separate piece of paper, break down your objective or destination into the tasks that you will need to perform before you can own your own restaurant, open a franchise, become an executive chef for a hotel, or write a book (for instance).

Now look at the tasks you've identified. Try to put them on a timeline to aid you in getting your career off and running. Remember to reevaluate this document from time to time. You may change your mind about your ultimate goals, and that's fine. As long as you have a plan in mind, it's easy to determine how to maximize the work you've already done and identify what needs to happen next.

If you are asked about your goals during an interview, be honest. If you intend to stay for a year, or until you have mastered a specific set of skills working for one person or company, let this be known up front. The company or person may still be able to work successfully with you, as long as you make clear why you are there and what your ultimate goal is.

Summary

The education that you will receive in this field is like a perpetual motion machine. It simply never ends. If you allow your training and education to end when you get your diploma or cordon bleu, you will be doing a grave disservice not only to yourself but to the entire profession as well.

There are countless ways to learn more, and most of them require no more exertion than reading books, magazines, and newspapers. Some of these activities, such as dining out and traveling, are so delightful as to make you wonder if you really should call them "learning experiences."

You will get back from your career almost exactly that which you have put into it. Any investment that you make in your education is an investment in your career and your future.

Culinary Schools and Related Educational Institutions

L'Academie de Cuisine
16006 Industrial Dr.
Gaithersburg, MD 20877-1414
lacademie.com

American River College
4700 College Oak Dr.
Sacramento, CA 95841
arc.losrios.cc.ca.us/~chef

Arizona Culinary Institute
10585 N. 114th St., #401
Scottsdale, AZ 85259
azculinary.com

Art Institute of Atlanta-Culinary Arts
6600 Peachtree Dunwoody Rd.
100 Embassy Row
Atlanta, GA 30328
aia.artinstitutes.edu

Art Institute of Houston-Culinary Arts
1900 Yorktown
Houston, TX 77056
aih.artinstitutes.edu

The Art Institute of New York City
75 Varick St.
New York, NY 10013
ainyc.aii.edu

The Art Institutes International Minnesota
15 S. Ninth St.
Minneapolis, MN 55402
aim.artinstitutes.edu

Atlantic Cape Community College
Academy of Culinary Arts
5100 Black Horse Pike
Mays Landing, NJ 08330-2699
atlantic.edu/aca

Baltimore International College
17 Commerce St.
Baltimore, MD 21202
bic.edu

Boston University Culinary Arts
808 Commonwealth Ave.
Boston, MA 02215
bu.edu/lifelong

California Culinary Academy
625 Polk St.
San Francisco, CA 94102
baychef.com

California School of Culinary Arts
521 E. Green St.
Pasadena, CA 91101
calchef.com

The Cambridge School of Culinary Arts
2020 Massachusetts Ave.
Cambridge, MA 02140-2104
cambridgeculinary.com

Capital Culinary Institute of Keiser College
1700 Halstead Blvd.
Tallahassee, FL 32308
capitalculinaryinstitute.com

Cascade Culinary Institute
2600 NW College Way
Bend, OR 97701
cocc.edu/culinary

Center for Culinary Arts
106 Sebethe Dr.
Cromwell, CT 06416
centerforculinaryarts.com

Colorado Mountain Culinary Institute
P.O. Box 10001SG
Glenwood Springs, CO 81602
coloradomtn.edu

Connecticut Culinary Institute
Talcott Plaza
230 Farmington Ave.
Farmington, CT 06032
ctculinary.com

Cook Street School of Fine Cooking
1937 Market St.
Denver, CO 80202
cookstreet.com

The Cooking and Hospitality Institute of Chicago
361 W. Chestnut
Chicago, IL 60610
chicnet.org

CULINARD, The Culinary Institute of Virginia College
65 Bagby Dr., Ste. 100
Birmingham, AL 35209
culinard.com

Culinary Institute Alain and Marie LeNôtre
7070 Allensby St.
Houston, TX 77022
lenotre-alain-marie.com

The Culinary Institute of America
1946 Campus Dr.
Hyde Park, NY 12538
ciachef.edu

DCT Swiss Hotel and Culinary Arts School
Halsdenstrasse 57
CH6002 Lucerne
Switzerland
http://culinaryschool.ch

Drexel University-Hospitality Management Department
Thirty-Third and Arch Sts., #110
Philadelphia, PA 19104
drexel.edu/hospitality

ESCF Groupe Ferrandi Bilingual Program
10 rue Poussin
Paris 75016
France
escf.ccip.fr

Faulkner State Community College
3301 Gulf Shores Pkwy.
Gulf Shores, AL 36542
faulkner.cc.al.us

Florida Culinary Institute
2400 Metrocentre Blvd.
West Palm Beach, FL 33407-9985
floridaculinary.com

The French Culinary Institute
462 Broadway
New York, NY 10013-2618
frenchculinary.com/shaw

French Pastry School
226 W. Jackson Blvd.
Chicago, IL 60606
frenchpastryschool.com

Grand Rapids Community College Hospitality Education
151 Fountain NE
Grand Rapids, MI 49503-3263
grcc.edu

Hillsborough Community College
4001 Tampa Bay Blvd.
Tampa, FL 33614
hcc.cc.fl.us

ICIF-USA
126 Second Pl.
Brooklyn, NY 11231
icif.com

The Illinois Institute of Art Chicago–Culinary Arts
180 N. Wabash
Chicago, IL 60601
ilic.artinstitutes.edu

The Institute of Culinary Education
50 W. Twenty-Third St.
New York, NY 10010
iceculinary.com

International School of Baking
1971 NW Juniper Ave.
Bend, OR 97701
schoolofbaking.com

Italian Institute for Advanced Culinary and Pastry Arts
Via T. Campanella, 37
Satriano, CZ 88060
Italy
italianculinary.it

JNA Institute of Culinary Arts
1212 S. Broad St.
Philadelphia, PA 19146
culinaryarts.com

Johnson and Wales University
College of Culinary Arts
8 Abbott Park Pl.
Providence, RI 02903
jwu.edu

The Kendall College School of Culinary Arts
2408 Orrington Ave.
Evanston, IL 60201
kendall.edu

Kura Hulanda Experience
Langestraat 8
Willemstad, Curaçao
Netherlands Antilles
kurahulanda.org

Le Cordon Bleu
8, rue Leon Delhomme
Paris 75015
France
http://cordonbleu.edu

Le Cordon Bleu at Atlantic Culinary Academy
23 Cataract Ave.
Dover, NH 03820
atlanticculinary.com

Le Cordon Bleu Australia
Days Rd., Regency Park
Adelaide 5010
Australia
cordonbleu.net/schools/default_au.htm

Le Cordon Bleu Culinary Program at Brown College
1440 Northland Dr.
Mendota Heights, MN 55120
chef-bc.com

Le Cordon Bleu Ottawa Culinary Arts Institute
453 Laurier Ave. E
Ottawa, ON K1N 6R4
Canada
http://lcbottawa.com

Le Cordon Bleu Schools, USA
2895 Greenpoint Pkwy., 6th Fl.
Hoffman Estates, IL 60195
lecordonbleuschoolsusa.com

Liaison College
2974 Lakeshore Blvd. W
Toronto, ON M8V 1J9
Canada
liaisoncollege.com

Los Angeles Trade-Technical College
Culinary Arts Dept.
400 W. Washington Blvd.
Los Angeles, CA 90015
lattc.cc.ca.us

Mississippi University for Women
Box W-1639
Columbus, MS 39701
muw.edu/interdisc

New England Culinary Institute
250 Main St.
Montpelier, VT 05602
neculinary.com

New England Culinary Institute at H. Lavity Stoutt
    Community College
P.O. Box 3097, Road Town
Tortola, British Virgin Islands
hlscc.edu.vg

New School Culinary Arts
131 W. Twenty-Third St.
New York, NY 10011
nsu.newschool.edu/culinary

New York University
Dept. of Nutrition and Food Studies
The Steinhardt School of Education
35 W. Fourth St., 10th Fl.
New York, NY 10012-1172
education.nyu.edu/food/shaw

Pacific Institute of Culinary Arts
1505 W. Second Ave.
Vancouver, BC V6H 3Y4
Canada
picachef.com

Pennsylvania College of Technology School of Hospitality
One College Ave.
Williamsport, PA 17701-5799
pct.edu

The Restaurant School at Walnut Hill College
4207 Walnut St.
Philadelphia, PA 19104
walnuthillcollege.com

San Diego Culinary Institute, Inc.
8024 La Mesa Blvd.
La Mesa, CA 91941
sdci-inc.com

San Jacinto College
8060 Spencer Hwy.
Pasadena, CA 77501-2007
sjcd.cc.tx.us

Sclafani's Cooking School, Inc.
107 Gennaro Pl.
Metairie, LA 70001-5209
sclafanicookingschool.com

Scottsdale Culinary Institute, a Le Cordon Bleu Program
8100 E. Camelback Rd., #1001
Scottsdale, AZ 85251
scichefs.com

Seattle Central Community College
Seattle Culinary Academy
1701 Broadway, Mailstop 2BE2120
Seattle, WA 98122
http://seattleculinary.com

Southern New Hampshire University Culinary Program
2500 N. River Rd.
Manchester, NH 03106
snhu.edu

Stratford University
School of Culinary Arts
7777 Leesburg Pike
Falls Church, VA 22043-2403
stratford.edu

Tante Marie School of Cookery
Woodham House, Carlton Rd.
Woking, Surrey GU21 4HF
England
tantemarie.co.uk

Texas Culinary Academy
11400 Burnet Rd., #2100
Austin, TX 78758
txca.com

United States Personal Chef Institute
481 Rio Rancho Blvd., Ste. B
Rio Rancho, NM 87124
uspci.com

Walt Disney World Center for Hospitality and Culinary Art
Valencia Community College, W. Campus
1800 S. Kerkman Rd.
Orlando, FL 32811
http://valencia.cc.fl.us

Western Culinary Institute
1316 SW Thirteenth Ave.
Portland, OR 97205
westernculinary.com

Culinary Journals, Magazines, and Newsletters

As you can see from the list that follows, there are many journals, magazines, and newsletters that you can read to help you find out more about the culinary career of your choice.

Professional Journals and Magazines

American Cake Decorating
P.O. Box 1385
Sterling, VA 20167-9806
cakemag.com

Art Culinaire
40 Mills St.
P.O. Box 9268
Morristown, NJ 07960
getartc.com

Baking with the American Harvest
626 Santa Monica Ave., #526
Santa Monica, CA 90401

Cheesemakers' Journal
85 Main St.
P.O. Box 85
Ashfield, MA 01330
info@cheesemaking.com

Chef
Talcott Communications Corp.
20 N. Wacker Dr., Ste. 3230
Chicago, IL 60606-3112
(This is a chef's business magazine.)

Chocolatier
Haymarket Group Ltd.
45 W. Thirty-Fourth St., Ste. 600
New York, NY 10001

Cooking for Profit
104 S. Main St., 7th Fl.
Fond du Lac, WI 54935
cookingforprofit.com/home_3.html

Culinary Trends
6285 E. Spring St., Ste. 107
Long Beach, CA 90808-9927
culinarytrends.net

Fancy Food
Talcott Communications Corp.
20 N. Wacker Dr., Ste. 3230
Chicago, IL 60606-3112
fancyfoodmagazine.com

Food Arts
Food Arts Publishing, Inc.
387 Park Ave. S
New York, NY 10016

Food for Health
15084 N. Ninety-Second Pl.
Scottsdale, AZ 85260

Fresh Cup Magazine
P.O. Box 82817
Portland, OR 97282-9961
freshcup.com

Gourmet Retailer
3301 Ponce de Leon Blvd., Ste. 300
Coral Gables, FL 33134
gourmetretailer.com

Health, Diet, and Nutrition
951 S. Oxford, No.109
Los Angeles, CA 90006

Journal of Culinary Practice
Food Products Press
10 Alice St.
Binghamton, NY 13904-1580

Journal of Gastronomy
America Institute of Food and Wine
1550 Bryant St., Ste. 700
San Francisco, CA 94103-4832

Journal of Home Economics
Association of Family and Consumer Science
1555 King St.
Alexandria, VA 22314

Journal of Italian Food and Wine
609 W. 114th St., Ste. 77
New York, NY 10125-0179

Kitchenware News
38 Lafayette St.
P.O. Box 1056
Yarmouth, ME 04096
kitchenwarenews.com

Macro Chef
243 Dickinson St.
Philadelphia, PA 19147

Magazine of La Cucina Italiana
230 Fifth Ave., Ste. 1111
New York, NY 10001
piacere.com

National Culinary Review
American Culinary Federation
P.O .Box 3466
San Bartoia Dr.
St. Augustine, FL 32085
acfchefs.org/pubs/ncr.html

Op Art International Gourmet Edition
German Marketing Services
206 W. Fifteenth St.
New York, NY 10011

Pastry Art and Design
Haymarket Group, Ltd.
45 W. Thirty-Fourth St., Ste. 600
New York, NY 10001
pastryartanddesign.com

Spain Gourmetour
Spanish Embassy Commerical Office
Ref: Spain Gourmetour
666 Fifth Ave.
New York, NY 10103
(A food, wine, and travel quarterly magazine)

Vegetarian Journal
Vegetarian Resource Group
P.O. Box 1463
Baltimore, MD 21203
vrg.org/journal

Wine Enthusiast
8 Saw Mill River Rd.
Hawthorne, NY 10532
wineenthusiast.com

Wine Spectator
387 Park Ave. S
New York, NY 10016
winespectator.com/wine/home

Zymurgy
P.O. Box 1679
Boulder, CO 80306-1679
(This is the journal of the American Homebrewers Association.)

General Interest Cooking Magazines

Adventures in Dining
P.O. Box W-1
Carmel, CA 93921

Ahimsa
American Vegan Society
P.O. Box H
Malaga, NJ 08328-0908
americanvegan.org

AIB Research Department Technical Bulletin
American Institute of Baking
1213 Bakers Way
Manhatten, KS 66502
aibonline.org

American Cake Decorating
P.O. Box 1385
Sterling, VA 20167-9806
cakemag.com

Asian Home Gourmet
Geyling, P.O. Box 0900
Singapore 9138
asianhomegourmet.com

Beer, The Magazine
P.O. Box 717
Hayward, CA 94543-0717

Better Homes and Gardens Eating Right, Living Well
Meredith Corp.
Special Interest Publications
1716 Locust St.
Des Moines, IA 50336
meredith.com

Bon Appetit
Condé Nast Publications
350 Madison Ave.
New York, NY 10017
condenast.co.uk

Brew
P.O. Box 1504
Martinez, CA 94553-9932

Chile Pepper
Out West Publishing
5106 Grand NE
P.O. Box 80780
Albuquerque, NM 87198
chilepepper.com

Cooking Light
P.O. Box 1748
Birmingham, AL 35201
cookinglight.com/cooking

Cook's Illustrated
Boston Common Press
17 Station St.
P.O. Box 569
Brookline, MA 02147-0569
cooksillustrated.com

Cuisine
Illustrated Guide to Creative Home Cooking
August Home Publishing
2200 Grand Ave
Des Moines, IA 50312
cuisinemagazine.com

Eating Well
Ferry Rd., P.O. Box 1001
Charlotte, VT 05445-1001
eatingwell.com

Energy Times
Nature's Plus
P.O. Box 91719
Long Beach, CA 90809-1719

FDA Consumer
Superintendent of Documents
P.O. Box 371954
Pittsburgh, PA 15250-7954
fda.gov/fdac/default.htm

Fine Cooking
The Taunton Press
63 S. Main St.
P.O. Box 5506
Newtown, CT 06470-9905
taunton.com/finecooking/index.asp

Food and Wine
American Express Pub. Co.
1120 Avenue of the Americas
New York, NY 10036
foodandwine.com

Global Gourmet
P.O. Box 3
Lakewood, NJ 08701

Good Taste
International Recipe Collection
4151 Knob Dr.
Eagan, MN 55122

Gourmet
Condé Nast
560 Lexington Ave.
New York, NY 10022-6876
http://eat.epicurious.com/gourmet

Herb Companion
Interweave Press
201 E. Fourth St.
Loveland, CO 80537
discoverherbs.com

Kitchen Garden
The Taunton Press
63 S. Main St.
P.O. Box 5506
Newtown, CT 06470-5506

Quick and Healthy Cooking
Rodale Press, Inc.
33 E. Minor St.
Emmaus, PA 18098

Saveur
100 Avenue of the Americas
New York, NY 10013-1605
saveur.com

Tea, A Magazine
P.O. Box 348
Scotland, CT 06264
teamag.com

Vegetarian Times
P.O. Box 570
Oak Park, IL 60303
vegetariantimes.com

Veggie Life
EGW Publishing Co.
1041 Shary Circle
Concord, CA 94520
veggielife.com

Weight Watchers Magazine
W/W Twentyfirst Corp.
360 Lexington Ave.
New York, NY 10017

Wine and Food Companion
P.O. Box 639
Lenox Hill Station
New York, NY 10021

Newsletters

American Herb Association Quarterly Newsletter
P.O. Box 1673
Nevada City, CA 95959

Art of Eating
P.O. Box 242
Peacham, VT 05862

Baking Sheet
King Arthur Flour Baker's Catalog
P.O. Box 876
Norwich, VT 05055-0876

Baking Update
Lallemand, Inc.
1620 Prefontaine
Montreal, QC H1W 2NB

Ball Consumer Newsletter
Alltrista Corp.
Direct Marketing, Dept. CN
P.O. Box 2005
Muncie, IN 47307-0005

Beard House Monthly
James Beard Foundation
167 W. Twelfth St.
New York, NY 10011

Calorie Control Commentary
Calorie Control Council
5775 Peachtree-Dunwoody Rd., Ste. 500-G
Atlanta, GA 30342

Cater Source Journal
P.O. Box 14776
Chicago, IL 60614

Consumer Magazines Digest: Nutrition and Food Related Health Topics
Consumer Choices, Inc.
1315 Lyons St.
Evanston, IL 60201

Cookbook Collector
1443 Sunset Dr.
Bogalusa, LA 70426

Cookbook Collector's Exchange
P.O. Box 32369
San Jose, CA 95152-2369

Cooking Contest Chronicle
P.O. Box 10792
Merrillville, IN 46411-0792

Cooking Contest Newsletter
P.O. Box 339
Summerville, SC 29484

Culinary Sleuth
P.O. Box 194
Bryn Mawr, PA 19010-0194

Food Channel
Nobel and Associates
515 N. State, 29th Fl.
Chicago, IL 60610

Food Forum
International Association of Culinary Professionals
304 W. Liberty St., Ste. 201
Louisville, KY 40202

Food History News
HC 60, Box 354A
Isleboro, ME 04848

Food and Nutrition
U.S. Department of Agriculture
Food and Nutrition Service
Alexandria, VA 22302

Food and Nutrition News
National Livestock and Meat Board
444 N. Michigan Ave.
Chicago, IL 60611

Foodtalk: The Newsletter for People Who Enjoy Food for the Mind as Well as the Table
P.O. Box 6543
San Francisco, CA 94101

Foodwatch Newsletter
Smithson Associates
6800 Galway Dr.
Edina, MN 55439

Fork, Fingers, and Chopsticks: Supporting Food, Nutrition, and Health Professionals in Multicultural Settings
Four Winds Food Specialists
P.O. Box 70015
Sunnyvale, CA 94086

GIG Newsletter
Gluten Intolerance Group of North America
P.O. Box 23053
Seattle, WA 98102-0353

Gluten Free Baker Newsletter
361 Cherrywood Dr.
Fairborn, OH 45324-4012

Gourmet News
United Publications
38 Lafayette St.
P.O. Box 1056
Yarmouth, ME 04096

Healthy Exchanges
P.O. Box 124
DeWitt, IA 52742-0124

Herb Gatherings
10949 E. 200 S
Lafayette, IN 47905-9453

Herb Quarterly
Long Mountain Press, Inc.
223 San Anselmo Ave., Ste. 7
San Anselmo, CA 94960

International Chili Society
P.O. Box 2966
Newport Beach, CA 92663

Issues in Vegetarian Dietetics
Lisa Ford, R.D., L.D.
9435 Haddington Ct.
Cincinnati, OH 45251

Jewish Vegetarians Newsletter
Jewish Vegetarians of North America
6938 Reliance Rd.
Federalsburg, MD 21632

Journal of Nutrition in Recipe and Menu Development
Haworth Press
10 Alice St.
Binghamton, NY 13904-7981

National Barbecue News
P.O. Box 981
Douglas, GA 51533

Nutrition Action Healthletter
Center for Science in the Public Interest
1875 Connecticut Ave. NW, Ste. 300
Washington, DC 20009-5728

Nutrition Bites
MKS Inc.
1259 El Camino Real, Ste. 1500
Menlo Park, CA 94025

Practical Vegetarian
P.O. Box 6253
Evanston, IL 60204

Seafood Source
National Fisheries Institute
1525 Wilson Blvd., Ste. 500
Arlington, VA 22209

Shitake News
Forest Resource Center
Route 2, Box 156A
Lanesboro, MN 55949-9648

Simple Cooking
P.O. Box 8
Steuben, ME 04680

Simply Seafood
Waterfront Press
1115 NW Forty-Sixth St.
Seattle, WA 98107

Tea Talk
R & R Publications
P.O. Box 860
Sausalito, CA 94966

U.S. Pastry Alliance
3349 Somerset Trace
Marietta, GA 30087

Vegetarian Journal's Food Service Update
Vegetarian Resource Group
P.O. Box 1463
Baltimore, MD 21203

Whole Food Journal
301 Thelma Dr., #508
Casper, WY 82609

Wine Advocate
P.O. Box 311
Monkton, MD 21111

Appendix C

Professional Food Organizations

American Culinary Federation, Inc.
P.O. Box 3466
10 San Bartola Dr.
St. Augustine, FL 32086
acfchefs.org

American Institute of Wine and Food
304 W. Liberty St., Ste. 201
Louisville, KY 40202
aiwf.org

Association of Chinese Cooking Teachers
c/o Martin Yan's Cooking School
1064-G Shell Blvd.
Foster City, CA 94404

Cooking Together Foundation
P.O. Box 149
Williamsburg, VA 23187-0149

International Association of Culinary Professionals
304 W. Liberty St., Ste. 201
Louisville, KY 40202
iacp.com

International Food, Wine, and Travel Writers Association
P.O. Box 13110
Long Beach, CA 90803
ifwtwa.org

James Beard Foundation
167 W. Twelfth St.
New York, NY 10011
jamesbeard.org

Les Dames d'Escoffier
3802 Jocelyn St. NW
Washington, DC 20015
ldei.org

Meals on Wheels America
mealsonwheels.org

National Restaurant Association
1200 Seventeenth St. NW
Washington, DC 20036
restaurant.org

Oldways Preservation and Exchange Trust
25 First St.
Cambridge, MA 02141
oldwayspt.org

Roundtable for Women in Foodservice
3022 W. Eastwood Ave.
Chicago, IL 60625

Share Our Strength
733 Fifteenth St. NW, Ste. 640
Washington, DC 20005
strength.org

Women Chefs and Restaurateurs
304 W. Liberty St., Ste. 201
Louisville, KY 40202
culinary.net

Recommended Readings

Adams, Jody, and Ken Rivard. *In the Hands of a Chef: Cooking with Jody Adams*. New York: William Morrow and Co., 2002.

Beard, James. *The James Beard Cookbook*, 3rd ed. New York: Marlowe and Co., 2002.

Bocuse, Paul. *Cuisine du Marche: en hommage à Alfred Guérot*. Flammarion, 1976.

Brillat-Savarin, Jean-Anthelme, and M.F.K. Fisher. *La Physiologie du Gout (The Physiology of Taste)*. Washington, D.C.: Counterpoint Press, 2000.

de Broglie, Marie-Blanche. *The Cuisine of Normandy*. Boston: Houghton Mifflin Co., 1984.

Bugialli, Giuliano. *The Fine Art of Italian Cooking*. New York: Times Books, 1990.

Casas, Penelope. *The Foods and Wines of Spain*, 11th ed. New York: Random House, 1982.

Child, Julia. *Mastering the Art of French Cooking*. New York: Knopf, 2001.

Claiborne, Craig. *The New York Times Cookbook*. New York: Times Books, 1979.

———. *A Feast Made for Laughter*. New York: Henry Holt, 1983.

Courtine, Robert J. *Grand Livre de la France à Table*. Delachaux and Niestlâe, 1982.

The Culinary Institute of America. *The Professional Chef*, 7th ed. The Culinary Institute of America, 2002.

David, Elizabeth. *Italian Food*, rev. ed. New York: Penguin, 1999.

———. *French Provincial Cooking*. New York: Penguin, 1999.

Dornenburg, Andrew, and Karen Page. *Becoming a Chef: With Recipes and Reflections from America's Leading Chefs*. New York: John Wiley and Sons, 1995.

———. *Culinary Artistry*. New York: John Wiley and Sons, 1996.

Escoffier, Georges Auguste. *Escoffier: Le Guide Culinaire*. C.H.I.P.S., 1979.

———. *Ma Cuisine*. A and W Publishing, 1979.

Febbroriello, Courtney. *Wife of the Chef*. New York: Clarkson Potter Publishers, 2003.

Franey, Pierre. *The New York Times More 60-Minute Gourmet*, reissue ed. New York: Fawcett Books, 1986.

———. *The New York Times 60-Minute Gourmet*. New York: Times Books, 2000.

Friberg, Bo. *The Professional Pastry Chef: Fundamentals of Baking and Pastry*, 4th ed. New York: John Wiley and Sons, 2002.

Gannon, Beverly, et al. *The Hali'Imaile General Store Cookbook: Homecooking from Maui*. Berkeley, Calif.: Ten Speed Press, 2001.

Gisslen, Wayne. *Professional Baking*, 3rd ed. New York: John Wiley and Sons, 2000.

————. *Professional Cooking*, 5th ed. New York: John Wiley and Sons, 2002.

Grigson, Jane. *The Observer Guide to European Cookery*. M. Joseph, 1983.

Guerard, Michel. *Cuisine Minceur*, reprint ed. New York: William Morrow and Co., 1986.

Hazan, Marcella. *The Classic Italian Cookbook*, reissue ed. New York: Ballantine Books, 1989.

Jaffrey, Madhur. *Madhur Jaffery's Indian Cookery*, expanded ed. Hauppauge, N.Y.: Barrons Educational Series, 1982.

Kaplan, Dorlene. *The Guide to Cooking Schools 2003: Cooking Schools, Courses, Vacations, Apprenticeships, and Wine Programs Throughout the World*, 15th ed. ShawGuides, 2002.

Karp, Karen, and Robert Wemischner. *Gourmet to Go: A Guide to Opening and Operating a Specialty Food Store*. New York: John Wiley and Sons, 1997.

Kennedy, Diana. *The Cuisines of Mexico*, rev. ed. New York: HarperCollins, 1989.

Labensky, Sarah R. *On Cooking: Techniques from Expert Chefs*, 3rd ed. Upper Saddle River, N.J.: Prentice Hall, 2002.

Labensky, Steven, et al. *Webster's New World Dictionary of Culinary Arts*, 2d ed. Pearson PTP, 2000.

Lagasse, Emeril. *Prime Time Emeril: More TV Dinners from America's Favorite Chef*. New York: William Morrow and Co., 2001.

Lawrence, Elizabeth. *The Complete Caterer: A Practical Guide to the Craft and Business of Catering*. New York: Doubleday, 1992.

Leeming, Margaret. *Chinese Regional Cookery*. North Pomfret, Vt.: Rider, 1987.

Liebling, A. J. *Between Meals: An Appetite for Paris*. New York: Modern Library, 1995.

Maximin, Jacques. *The Cuisine of Jacques Maximin*. New York: William Morrow and Co., 1986.

Medecin, Jacques. *Cuisine Niçoise*. New York: Penguin, 1991.

Moisimann, Anton. *Cuisine à la Carte*. CBI Publishing Co., 1981.

———. *Anton Moisimann's Fish Cuisine*. Humanity Press, 1988.

Montagne, Prosper. *Larousse Gastronomique*, rev. ed. New York: Clarkson Potter, 2001.

Revel, Jean-Francois. *Culture and Cuisine*. DeCapo Press, 1984.

Roden, Claudia. *A New Book of Middle Eastern Food*, rev. ed. New York: Knopf, 2000.

Root, Waverley. *The Food of Italy*, reissue ed. New York: Vintage Books, 1971.

Rosso, Julee. *The Silver Palate Cookbook*. New York: Workman Publishing Company, 1982.

Roux, Albert, and Michel Roux. *The New Classic Cuisine*. Hauppauge, N.Y.: Barrons Educational Series, 1984.

Ruhlman, Michael. *The Making of a Chef: Mastering Heat at the Culinary Institute*. New York: Owl Books, 1999.

Senderens, Alain. *The Three-Star Recipes of Alain Senderens*, reprint ed. New York: William Morrow and Co., 1982.

Treuille, Eric, and Jeni Wright. *Le Cordon Bleu Complete Cooking Techniques: The Indispensable Reference Demonstrates over 700 Illustrated Techniques with 2,000 Photos and 200 Recipes*. New York: William Morrow and Co., 1997.

Troisgros, Jean, and Pierre Troisgros. *The Nouvelle Cuisine of Jean and Pierre Troisgros*. New York: William Morrow and Co., 1978.

Verge, Roger. *The Cuisine of the South of France*. New York:
    William Morrow and Co., 1985.
Waters, Alice. *The Chez Panisse Menu Cookbook*. New York:
    Random House, 1985.
Wolfert, Paula. *Couscous and Other Good Food from Morocco*. New
    York: HarperCollins, 1973.
———. *Mediterranean Cooking*, rev. ed. New York: Ecco, 1994.

About the Author

Mary Deirdre Donovan has been a practicing member of the culinary arts for the past twenty-two years. Her first jobs included working at a small country club and as a student working in a college cafeteria. From fast-food outlets to fine dining establishments, front of the house, back of the house, and even management, she has had an opportunity to experience a number of different positions.

As food writer and editor, she has learned about another side of the industry: education, writing, photography, video, traditional publishing, and multimedia programs.

She has done food styling for various books and magazines, tested and developed recipes, and helped to develop a recipe management software program. Mary acts as the master of ceremonies for cooking demonstrations and has appeared on television and National Public Radio in the role of "culinary pop diva."

In her spare time, she cooks and gardens with her family—Thomas, Connor, Bronwyn, Molly, and Daphne—in the beautiful mid-Hudson Valley.